"Someone is killing off the jurors. You're the next name on the list."

As Michael's words sank into her consciousness, Brooke's blue eyes widened.

"You're talking about a serial killer here in Colorado."

"Yes."

"And he's coming after me?"

"I'm sorry, Brooke." He loosened his grip on her arms, putting his right hand on her shoulder.

She wrenched free. "Why do you care? This is my life. I'll take care of myself." The woman was trying desperately to keep it together. He couldn't blame her for that.

As she turned on her heel and marched toward the stairs, he gave her points for spirit and guts.

But she was way out of her league.

It was up to him to make sure she stayed alive.

CASSIE MILES

CHRISTMAS CRIME *in* COLORADO

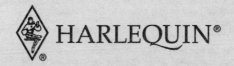

TORONTO • NEW YORK • LONDON
AMSTERDAM • PARIS • SYDNEY • HAMBURG
STOCKHOLM • ATHENS • TOKYO • MILAN • MADRID
PRAGUE • WARSAW • BUDAPEST • AUCKLAND

With love to the handsome and brilliant
Finn Hayden Bergstrom-Glaser.
And, as always, to Rick.

Recycling programs
for this product may
not exist in your area.

ISBN-13: 978-0-373-69369-6
ISBN-10:   0-373-69369-9

CHRISTMAS CRIME IN COLORADO

Copyright © 2008 by Kay Bergstrom

Printed in U.S.A.

ABOUT THE AUTHOR

Though born in Chicago and raised in Los Angeles, Cassie Miles has lived in Colorado long enough to be considered a semi-native. The first home she owned was a log cabin in the mountains overlooking Elk Creek with a thirty mile commute to her work at the *Denver Post*.

After raising two daughters and cooking tons of macaroni and cheese for her family, Cassie is trying to be more adventurous in her culinary efforts. Ceviche, anyone? She's discovered that almost anything tastes better with wine. A lot of wine. When she's not plotting Harlequin Intrigue books, Cassie likes to hang out at the Denver Botanical Gardens near her high-rise home.

Books by Cassie Miles

HARLEQUIN INTRIGUE
  832—ROCKY MOUNTAIN MANEUVERS*
  874—WARRIOR SPIRIT
  904—UNDERCOVER COLORADO**
  910—MURDER ON THE MOUNTAIN**
  948—FOOTPRINTS IN THE SNOW
  978—PROTECTIVE CONFINEMENT†
  984—COMPROMISED SECURITY†
  999—NAVAJO ECHOES
1025—CHRISTMAS COVER-UP
1048—MYSTERIOUS MILLIONAIRE
1074—IN THE MANOR WITH THE MILLIONAIRE
1102—CHRISTMAS CRIME IN COLORADO

*Colorado Crime Consultants
**Rocky Mountain Safe House
†Safe House: Mesa Verde

CAST OF CHARACTERS

Brooke Johnson—Escaping from a devastating divorce, she finds solace in Aspen, Colorado... until her look-alike roommate is murdered.

Michael Shaw—This police detective from Alabama comes west to avenge the murder of his best friend and to protect others from a serial killer.

Sally Klinger—Brooke's roommate was a good-time girl and expert snowboarder. Did her resemblance to Brooke lead to her murder?

Thomas Johnson—Brooke's former husband, a D.A. in Atlanta, still bears a grudge against his ex-wife.

Robby Lee Warren—Convicted of a petty crime, he was murdered in prison.

Jackson Warren—The older brother of Robby Lee has sworn revenge on the jury that convicted his brother.

Tyler Hennessey—A superstar snowboarder who claims to have loved Sally. But his mercurial temper gets him in trouble.

Peter Thorne—He might know more than he's saying.

Damien Klinger—Sally's estranged husband is glad to have her out of his life.

Hannah Lewis—The owner of the boutique where Brooke works. She has everyone's best interests at heart.

Chapter One

In early December, night came quickly to the snow-covered hills and valleys of the high Rockies. The sunset faded. Dusk blew across the land, bending the bare branches of white aspens and tall pines. Stars began to appear. Outside her A-frame house, Brooke Johnson stood beside her Jeep station wagon and listened to the sibilant breeze. *Shush, shush, time to rest, to sleep, to heal. Shush.*

Less than four months ago, she'd packed up and moved from Atlanta to Aspen, Colorado. Leaving behind friends and a corporate job in human resources, she sought solace in the big-shouldered Rockies where no one knew her history. Her ex-husband Thomas. His infidelities. Her restraining orders. The miscarriage. The humiliation of a marriage gone terribly wrong.

In Aspen, Brooke hoped to make a fresh start at age thirty-two. Though she'd only visited Colorado twice before, she thought of the mountains as a natural paradise—a Shangri-la where the air was clean and dreams came true. She'd found a job at a boutique and spent a sizable chunk of her savings on the security deposit for this furnished A-frame nestled on the sunny side of a canyon. From where she stood, she could only see the rooftops of two other houses. Both were vacant during the week, used only on weekends and holidays when the families came up to ski. She liked the solitude, the silence behind the wind. But the magnificence of the Aspen environs came at a steep price; the astronomical rent meant that Brooke had to have a roommate.

And that was her current problem: her roommate, Sally Klinger.

When they first met, Sally joked about how lucky they were to have the same build, same coloring and same long, dark auburn hair and blue eyes.

"Why lucky?" Brooke had asked.

"Because all the clothes that look good on you will suit me just fine!"

Sally took their physical similarity as an open invitation to help herself to Brooke's wardrobe. Brooke quickly realized that this was a minor annoyance compared to Sally's constant cursing, her blaring music and her clutter—magazines, dirty dishes, shoes and clothes—strewn with abandon around the house. Not to mention her herd of boyfriends, some of whom felt free to wander through the house in nothing more than boxer shorts.

Brooke had spoken to her dozens of times to no effect. This roommate thing just wasn't working. Sally had to go.

Standing on the long, level driveway that branched off from the steep road leading up the side of the canyon, Brooke glared toward the A-frame. Every light was lit, including the lamp in her own bedroom—a probable indication that her roommate had been "borrowing" more clothes. Sally's SUV was parked facing the road, ready to zoom the roughly twelve miles into town to troll for ski bums and beer.

Tonight, Brooke would tell her roommate that she'd had

enough. She hadn't escaped from her ex-husband only to fall into another abusive living arrangement. Even though Sally was only a roommate, Brooke intended to break up with her. It had to be done.

She turned the handle on the back door which was, of course, unlocked in spite of Sally's promise to keep the place secure. As soon as Brooke stepped inside, she wrinkled her nose in disgust. It smelled even worse than usual in here. The kitchen counter was littered with beer bottles and two plates with half-eaten sandwiches. *Two* plates. Very likely, Sally was upstairs in her bedroom with yet another boyfriend.

Dropping her backpack amid the junk on the kitchen table, Brooke listened. Instead of the usual screeches of passion that indicated Sally was entertaining, she heard silence. No music. No TV. Not even the sound of Sally yakking.

"Sally? Are you home?"

She had to be here. Her car was parked outside.

"Sally?"

Brooke entered the living room where the sloped ceiling peaked at the top of the A. She stopped short. Denim-clad legs and bare feet dangled above her head. Sally hung by her neck from a rope.

Brooke stumbled backward, banging into the sofa. Her gut clenched, and she doubled over. *This isn't happening. This can't be happening.*

It was only an illusion—her mind had to be playing tricks on her. Her anger at Sally had somehow caused this waking nightmare.

She didn't want Sally dead, only gone from her house. Brooke forced herself to breathe slowly, the way her therapist had shown her as a way to control her fears.

Slowly, inhale and exhale. She grounded herself. Then, she looked up.

Brooke's gaze slid down the rope to Sally, who wore a white shirt, jeans and Brooke's new down vest. On her pale wrist was the delicate Cartier watch Brooke's father had given her when she graduated from college. She couldn't see Sally's face from where she was—her long, auburn hair spilled forward.

A scream clawed up the back of Brooke's throat, but she held back. *Control. I need to control my mind, control my fear.* But how could she? Inside her head, rational thought tumbled into an incoherent whirl. She couldn't make sense of this horror, feeling like she'd stepped onto a movie set where the director would yell "Cut," and Sally would be fine. Yet she still hung there. Dead weight.

Maybe not dead. Not yet. Though unconscious, Sally might still be alive. The thought spurred Brooke into action. She leapt forward, wrapping her arms around Sally's legs, trying to boost her up. Her bare feet were ice-cold. Her body twisted and swung. With a horrible thud, her back hit the wall below the railing.

This wasn't working; Brooke needed help. In the kitchen, she grabbed her cell phone from her backpack and called 911. While waiting for an answer, she raced back to the front room and climbed the open staircase to the balcony.

When the 911 operator answered, Brooke blurted out, "An ambulance. My roommate. She tried to hang herself."

"Ma'am, I need your location."

She rattled off the address as she stared at the knot in the thick, heavy braided rope. She tugged at the loose end that coiled by her feet, then clawed at the tangled snarl looped around the railing. With Sally's weight pulling the rope taut, there was no way she could untie the knot.

"Stay on the line," the operator said. "Tell me what you're doing."

"The rope," Brooke said. "I have to cut the rope."

"An ambulance is on the way. Is your roommate conscious? Is she—"

"No." She went down the staircase, her thick-soled hiking boots jolting her legs with each step. "I know CPR. If I can get her down, I can help her."

In the kitchen, she pulled a butcher knife from the wood block near the sink. It would take forever to saw through that thick rope with a blade this flimsy. She needed something heavier.

Outside the kitchen door under the eaves was a waist-high box that held a cord of wood for the fireplace and an ax. She dropped her cell phone on the table and hurried out the back door. Her hands trembled as she hefted the ax onto her shoulder.

Panic magnified her senses. The light above the back door shone with an intense silvery luster—a contrast to the pitch-black shadows of night. Over the rush of her own breathing, she heard a rustling in the branches followed by the crunch of footsteps on the snow. Turning toward the sound, she peered into a thick chokecherry bush that rose higher than the top of her head. "Is someone there?" she asked, her voice unsteady with fear.

The lights from the house reflected in a pair of eyes. No more than fifteen feet away, they stared at her through a bare thicket, then blinked and were gone.

Sheer terror washed over her. Had she actually seen something? Those eyes didn't even look human.

More loudly, she demanded, "Who's there?"

The wind blew, and the shadows shifted. She heard no other sound, saw nothing. She had no time to search. Her focus came back to a single purpose: Get Sally down.

Carrying the ax, she ran back into the house, closed the door and locked it behind her. Unable to forget those weirdly shining eyes, she moved cautiously through the galley-style kitchen. Her rational mind was clamoring to be heard over the terror.

Hyperaware of every sound and every shadow, Brooke edged into the front room. The plain, simple furniture didn't offer many hiding places. She scanned the patterned blue sofas and the rocking chairs by the fireplace. She was dimly aware of a terrible smell, a smell that said there was no rush to get Sally down because she was already gone.

And then she saw him. Silhouetted against the sliding glass doors, he darted across the deck at the front of the house. Then he was gone.

Her pulse hammered. Her blood rushed, and she felt dizzy.

Outside the sliding glass doors, the outline of a man took shape again. Her eyes narrowed in a squint, but she couldn't see him clearly. The lines of his shoulders shifted like a mirage.

Illusion or reality? Either she was being threatened by an intruder—a killer?—or she'd lost her mind.

The wind blew, and the glass trembled. The man reached for the door handle. She prayed the doors were locked. No such luck. The glass inched open.

"Stay back!" She stepped forward and away from Sally's dangling legs. Brooke swung the ax in a wide arc. "Don't come in here!"

She heard a hissing noise. The sound of breathing? He was gasping like the flatlanders who weren't accustomed to the altitude. He was someone who had come from far away.

Her ex-husband.

That can't be! I've left that part of my life behind. Thomas wouldn't come here. He wouldn't dare.

"Show yourself!" she yelled at the man. There was no way she could fight a shadow or a nightmare illusion. If she saw him, she could fight back. Damn it, she had an ax. She wasn't helpless.

Unless he has a gun.

She crept forward, holding the ax at the ready. The handle slipped in her sweaty palms. She tightened her grip.

A face pressed up against the window. The features were unclear. All she could really see were the eyes—hate-filled eyes glaring into her soul.

No time to think. No point in screaming. She dropped the ax, pivoted and ran. She'd heard his gasps. He was already out of breath. She might be able to outdistance him.

Racing through the kitchen, she glanced at her cell phone on the table. Where the hell was the ambulance? The police? She flipped the lock on the door, grabbed the butcher knife off the counter and dove into the night.

Her hiking boots slowed her down, but the heavy soles had good traction in the packed snow. She ran down the driveway, passing her Jeep. *Damn it! Why didn't I grab my car keys instead of a butcher knife?* She wasn't thinking clearly. Her perceptions were all wrong. That one mistake—knife instead of car keys—could get her killed.

She saw headlights on the road leading up the steep cliff. The car turned at her driveway. It had to be the police. But why weren't they using the siren?

A bronze SUV pulled in and parked. A tall man in a brown leather bomber jacket and jeans stepped out of the driver's side.

She whirled and peered back at the well-lit house. The intruder was nowhere in sight. Had she even seen him? She could have imagined him, creating a vision that matched her fears. It wouldn't be the first time. She hated the fact that she couldn't always trust her own eyes.

After she left Thomas, she'd had nightmares so intense that she went to a therapist and got a prescription, which seemed to make things worse. More than once, she woke in a cold sweat, screaming. Those vivid, Technicolor illusions felt more tangible than her everyday life. She'd seen danger on every street corner, heard threats in every utterance. Thinking of that terror, she could taste the familiar coppery bite of fear on her tongue. Her lungs ached with the pressure of controlling her panic.

Spinning around, she faced the tall man who stood beside his car. He appeared real. His lips moved, and he spoke.

"What's the problem?"

If he had to ask, he hadn't come in response to her 911 call. When he took a step toward her, she held up the knife. "Stay where you are. What's your name?"

"Michael Shaw." The glow from his headlights showed a calm, self-assured expression. His face was familiar. "We've met. I was hoping you'd remember me," he said with a hint of a Southern drawl. "I was in your shop this afternoon. You sold me a pair of gloves."

Indeed, she recalled. And the memory—a reality—grounded her.

Michael Shaw had been the high point of her day. He was tall and lean with eyes the color of jade and a smile that could melt a glacier. She'd been flattered when he leaned across the counter in the boutique and asked her opinion as if he really cared what she thought. They must have talked for fifteen minutes. Unfortunately, his accent reminded her of Atlanta—the one place in the world she wanted to forget.

When he'd asked her out for coffee, she'd treasured the moment but still said no. After Thomas, she'd had enough of smooth-talking Southern gentlemen to last the rest of her lifetime.

"Why are you here?" she demanded. "Did you follow me?"

"Calm down, Brooke. I'm a cop. Remember? I told you this afternoon. I'm a police detective from Birmingham, Alabama."

She nodded, recalling their conversation. He was a cop. That didn't necessarily mean he wasn't a threat. "What do you want from me?"

"We need to talk. I have something important to tell you, and it can't wait any longer," he said, his eyes falling on the knife she held.

"That's why you asked me out."

"And you turned me down." He clapped one gloved hand upon his chest. "Nearly broke my heart."

He took a step toward her, and she pointed the knife directly at his chest. "Don't come any closer."

"Okay, Brooke." He stepped back and paused, studying her. "You want to tell me what's wrong? Maybe I can help."

Suspiciously, she studied his handsome features. He seemed not to know what was going on, yet he happened to arrive at her house at this particular moment *by pure chance.* Could she trust him? After being stalked by her ex, she'd learned not to trust in coincidence. On the other hand, she needed help.

"It's Sally," she said. "My roommate."

"Tell me about Sally." His voice was steady and reassuring, just the right tone for a cop. Not that she was entirely sure she trusted cops, either. "You don't have to be afraid. Whatever it is, I'm on your side."

She stared into the darkness at the end of the driveway. Her ears strained to hear the sound of an approaching siren. "The police are on the way. The *real* police."

"Oh, I'm a real officer. If you want, I'll show you my badge."

"That's not necessary."

"Okay." He nodded. "Now, take a breath. A long, slow breath. You need to calm down, Brooke."

His tone irritated her, somehow implying that her terror was silly. "Don't patronize me."

"I'm sorry. I didn't mean to. I just want you to tell me what's got you so scared."

My whole life. But she didn't have time to explain. She had to cut Sally down, and she needed Michael to help her. "Do you have a gun?"

"Yes."

"Follow me."

Aware that she might be making another mistake in judgment, she led Michael to the kitchen door of the A-frame. Was there any hope that Sally could be saved? Of course there was, she told herself.

He held his gun in both hands and pushed open the door with his foot. "Is someone in there with your roommate?"

"I thought I saw him. A face at the window."

"Stay close to me."

He entered with the kind of confidence that comes from

training, identifying himself loudly and repeatedly as a policeman. His deep voice echoed against the slanted walls of the house. The barrel of his gun was pointed and ready.

When he saw Sally, he paused. "Your roommate?"

"Yes."

"She looks a lot like you."

Chapter Two

Reaching up, Michael grasped the wrist of the woman who hung from the heavy rope, trying to find a pulse. Nothing. Not even a flutter. Her skin felt as cold as a gutted trout. She smelled like feces. In his ten years on the Birmingham PD, Michael had only seen one other hanging. But he didn't need a coroner to tell him this woman was deceased.

He glanced toward Brooke. Though she stood very still with the butcher knife clutched in her fist, her blue eyes were alive, darting in restless panic.

"We need to cut her down," she said in a shaky voice. "She might just be unconscious. I know CPR."

He suspected that she already knew her roommate was dead, but he didn't feel it was the moment to state that painful truth out loud. "You said there was someone else in the house."

"I think so." She pointed toward the sliding glass doors. "Over there. I think he was dressed in black."

"Gloves?"

"I don't know."

"How tall?"

"Don't know. Average."

"Did you recognize him?" She refused to look directly at him. "What aren't you telling me?"

"It was all too fast." Her features twisted in anguish. "I'm not sure he was really there."

It took guts to admit that she was freaked out, but he hoped her possible delusion wasn't symptomatic. "Has that happened to you before? Seeing things that aren't there?"

"Yes."

"Are you taking any medications?"

Her chin lifted. "We don't have time to talk about any of that. We need to help Sally."

Whether she was delusional or not, she was in serious denial about Sally's condition. He wished that he knew more about Brooke Johnson, that he'd taken more time to research her personal history before he'd tracked her down. "First, we need to make sure there's no one else in the house. I want you to come with me. We'll start upstairs."

Holding his gun at the ready, he climbed the staircase with Brooke right behind him. When he pushed open the door to the first bedroom, he saw chaos. Unmade bed. Curtains torn askew. Dirty dishes piled on the bedside table. Clothes draped everywhere. "Could be there was a struggle in here."

"Actually," Brooke said, "this is the way it always looks."

Michael nodded, making a mental note to search Sally's cluttered desktop later for a suicide note. "Okay, let's check the other rooms."

At the opposite end of the open balcony was Brooke's neat room—a major contrast to the chaos left behind by her roommate. The open door of her closet revealed a neat row of plastic hangers with all the shirts facing the same direction. From the clean surface of her dresser and her desk with a closed laptop to the autumnal quilt on her double bed, this space reflected someone who valued order. When she reached down to straighten the brown rug on the hardwood floor beside the bed, he stopped her.

"Don't touch anything. This is a crime scene."

Her spine stiffened as if offended by his statement. "This is my home. It's supposed to be a place where I feel safe."

With her thick reddish-brown hair and delicate features, she was a whole lot more attractive than her driver's license photo. Other than that obvious observation, he didn't know what to make of Ms. Brooke Johnson. Though she was upset, she hadn't lost control, which showed an admirable strength of character. On the other hand, she might have seen a man who wasn't there.

She held herself with an aloof poise. Cool, but not cold—not an ice princess. Earlier today, when he talked to her at that high-priced accessory boutique, she'd been friendly, even laughed at his lame jokes. He'd liked her enough that he'd held off telling her why he sought her out. He had wanted to wait, to build trust. Now, he feared that his hesitation might have proved fatal for her roommate. If he had to guess, he would say that Sally's death was not a suicide.

The wail of an approaching ambulance siren cut through the night. He looked toward the window. "The paramedics will be here real soon."

She stepped into the hallway and leaned her back against the wall, her gaze fastened on the heavy rope tied around the banister. "She's dead, isn't she?"

"There's nothing you could have done to save her."

"I was so angry at her. She was driving me crazy with her clutter and her idiot boyfriends. I couldn't stand it anymore." Her words gushed out. Like a confession. "When I came home tonight, I was going to confront her. She had to shape up or get out. I should have been more understanding. I should have tried harder."

"This isn't your fault, Brooke."

What he was about to tell her would make her feel a lot worse than she did right now, but there was no way to avoid the truth. The police would be here in minutes, and Michael was obligated to give them an explanation for why he'd shown up on Brooke's doorstep.

He holstered his gun and stepped in front of her. "I want you to listen to me. Listen carefully."

"Why is this happening? Why?"

"Brooke, look at me."

When she lifted her face, he saw confusion and anger. He wished there was time to be gentle, but he'd missed that opportunity. "Three years ago in Atlanta," he said, "you were on a jury."

"What?" She shook her head as if his words were incomprehensible.

"You have to remember."

"Don't tell me what to do." He stepped back, aware that she still had the knife. "I don't know who you are. Don't care what you have to say."

"You've got to hear this."

"Leave me alone."

When she started toward the stairs, he easily grabbed her wrist and gave it a flick. The butcher knife clattered to the hardwood floor. He held both her arms, forcing her to stand still. "Listen to me."

Her teeth bared in a snarl. "Let go of me."

"Do you remember the trial?"

"Armed robbery," she snapped. "The guy was guilty."

"His name was Robert E. Lee Warren, known as Robby Lee. Six weeks ago, he was killed in a prison fight."

"Why are you telling me this?" The ambulance siren was right outside the door. The emergency lights flashed against the walls of the living room.

"You were juror number four," he said. "The first three people on that jury list are dead."

"I don't understand."

"Someone is killing off the jurors who convicted Robby Lee. You're the next name on that list."

As his words sank into her consciousness, the fight seemed to drain from her body. Her blue eyes widened. "You're talking about a serial killer."

"Yes."

"And he's coming after me?"

"I'm sorry, Brooke." He loosened his grip on her arms, putting his right hand on her shoulder.

She wrenched free. "Why do you care? This is my life. I'll take care of myself."

As she turned on her heel and marched toward the stairs, he gave her points for spirit and guts. But she was way out of her league.

It was up to him to make sure she stayed alive.

BROOKE HUDDLED in the backseat of Deputy George McGraw's spotless SUV. Her fingers were wrapped tightly around a mug of herbal tea that had gone cold as she stared at her house. So much for a safe haven. As Michael had so calmly pointed out, her A-frame was a crime scene.

She rubbed at her bare wrist, wishing that she'd worn

her watch when she left the house this morning. The gold Cartier with the cream-colored face had been taken away with Sally's body in an ominously silent ambulance. Brooke had no idea how much time had passed since the police arrived. It seemed like only minutes, but it must have been longer—much longer. So much had happened. Deputy McGraw had taken her statement. Official vehicles had arrived and departed. Right now, there were several officers tromping up and down the steep hills and forest surrounding her house, waving flashlights and snapping photographs.

Her jaw clenched as she watched. She wanted them all to leave. Her preferred method for coping with stress was to hide away *by herself* and find something to keep her hands busy. Her fingers itched to do something useful. Busywork. Instead of sitting here, mired in worry, she wanted to start cleaning. She'd scrub every surface in the house, wash her roommate's dirty dishes, pack up her belongings and send them to…where? She drew a blank, unable to recall if Sally had ever mentioned where she came from, or her parents' address, or even if she had brothers and sisters.

Sadness welled up inside her. Her roommate had lived in the moment with the volume cranked up high. For Sally, every word was a song. Every step, a dance. She partied all night and still had enough energy to go hiking at dawn. But that was all Brooke really knew about her.

As Brooke stared toward the house, her vision blurred with rising tears. She should have paid more attention to Sally, should have appreciated her exuberant appetite for life instead of complaining about the noise.

Outside the back door that led to her kitchen, she saw Deputy McGraw conferring with Michael, who had been readily accepted by the local officers as soon as he showed his badge. He glanced toward her with his cool jade eyes, his thumb hitched in the pocket of his jeans next to the holster on his belt.

She was still angry about their confrontation outside her bedroom. He'd knocked the knife from her hands, grabbed her arms without permission; she'd be well within her rights to charge him with assault.

But she hadn't been harmed. And he'd touched her with strength, not cruelty. Instinctively, she knew he didn't want to hurt her. He was there to help. When he'd forced her to listen to him, she saw the worry in his expression—a deep and abiding concern for her safety. For an instant, she'd wanted to accept his protection and take shelter in his arms.

Then sanity had returned. She didn't know anything about this guy and didn't want to believe his story about someone killing jurors from that trial three years ago. It didn't make sense. If there really was such a serial killer, the FBI would investigate, wouldn't they?

She'd be nuts to trust this good-looking cop from Alabama. The fact that Michael had come all the way across the country to warn her was decidedly strange. Why hadn't he just picked up the phone and called? Now that he'd delivered the information, what did he intend to do?

The car door opened, and Deputy McGraw climbed inside. A huge, barrel-chested man with a walrus mustache, he took up a lot of space as he settled on the backseat beside her and closed the door.

"How are you holding up, Brooke?"

"I have some questions." She forced herself to stay calm, kept all the turmoil hidden inside.

"Maybe I can give you some answers," McGraw rumbled in a deep, gravelly voice. "Go ahead and ask."

"When I first saw Sally, I thought she might be…" She

pushed the thought away before a clear memory could take shape. "Was there anything I could have done?"

"According to the coroner, her neck snapped and she died immediately. You couldn't have saved her."

Not unless I'd been here. Not unless I'd been more understanding, more protective. "Was it suicide?"

"Did she seem depressed? Nervous?"

She shook her head. "Did you know Sally?"

"Gave her a speeding ticket once. She was a real live wire. Maybe a little bit of a party girl." Though he growled, like rocks in a tumbler, there was no animosity in his tone. "Did Sally Klinger have a lot of boyfriends?"

"Oh, yeah."

"Anybody special?"

She concentrated, remembering a parade of tanned, outdoorsy young men. "There was one. Streaky blond hair. A tattoo of a lightning bolt on his wrist. Tyler?"

"Tyler Hennessey? The X Games snowboarder?"

"That sounds right. Sally was teaching snowboarding at the ski school." She'd suggested that Brooke try snowboarding in addition to her beginner skiing lessons. Joking, Sally had promised to show her the "ups and downs" of snowboarding. "Why would she kill herself? She seemed to love her life here."

"You knew her better than I did."

"We didn't really get along, to be honest," Brooke said.

There was no point in sugarcoating their relationship. Just this afternoon, she'd been complaining about her roommate to Hannah Lewis, the owner of the boutique where she worked. Guiltily, Brooke remembered saying that she could just kill Sally.

The deputy cleared his throat. "Did your roommate ever mention her husband?"

Brooke gasped. "Sally was married?"

"I'm guessing they're separated. His residence is Denver, but we haven't been able to reach him."

The fact that Sally had a husband made it seem possible that she'd been murdered as part of a love triangle. A jealous husband might want revenge on his wayward wife. "You never answered my question about suicide."

"I won't have a definite answer until after we've done a bit more investigating." The big man settled back in his seat and exhaled, frowning. Beneath his mustache, he frowned. "Looks like suicide. She could've slung the rope around her neck and jumped."

Not something Brooke wanted to think about. She suppressed a shudder.

"But I'm not so sure," McGraw said. "For one thing, she didn't leave a note. For another, there's your statement. You said you might have seen a man outside the sliding glass doors."

"He didn't speak." On that point, she was clear. "Did you find footprints on the deck?"

"Sorry, Brooke. This snow is half mush and half ice. If we'd had a nice coat of new snow, we would have had a better shot at corroborating your story. Tell me about the guy again."

"He seemed to be wearing black. I thought he started to open the sliding glass doors." She hated to think of herself so caught up in a delusion that she'd threatened the air with an axe. "I wish I could give you a better description. I was scared."

"You must have been relieved when Detective Shaw turned up. He seems like a decent guy."

"Has he told you about the serial killer?"

The deputy nodded. "Heck of a thing."

It seemed that Deputy McGraw believed Michael's story. Of course, he would. Lawmen always stuck together as a matter of professional courtesy. When she'd taken out a restraining order against her ex-husband—a district attorney—the police didn't believe her. They stood behind Thomas in a solid blue wall and made her feel like a nutcase.

Irritated, she said, "I thought the FBI handled serial killer investigations."

"That's right. I put in a call to the Denver office."

"Why?"

"We need to consider all the possibilities. Let's just suppose that Michael's theory is right on target. A killer coming after you might have mistakenly attacked Sally. You two gals look enough alike to be sisters."

Brooke closed her eyes. Had Sally died in her place? Was Sally's death her fault? Her shoulders slumped, weighed down beneath a mantle of guilt.

"Are you okay?" McGraw asked.

No. I'll never be okay again. She couldn't allow herself to believe that she was responsible for Sally's death. She had to stay in control. In a small voice, she said, "I'm fine."

"You've been through a lot tonight. Suicide is bad enough. But murder?" He shook his head. "Heck of a thing."

"Yes," she whispered.

"We're treating this investigation like a homicide. That's why there's a swarm of officers up here, taking fingerprints and photos, marking off anything that might be evidence."

She looked through the windshield at the officers, all busy with different tasks. She imagined them upstairs in her bedroom, pawing through her drawers, looking over her personal things. "When can I get back into my house?"

"Not tonight," he said. "Is there somebody you can stay with? You work for Hannah Lewis, don't you?"

"Yes."

"Maybe you can stay with Hannah. I'm sure she's got an extra room."

"I'll be fine." Brooke suddenly felt desperate to get away from all the flashing lights and crackling radios. "Is it all right if I leave now?"

"I'll have one of my men bring your backpack. Is there anything else you want from the house?"

Everything. An outfit to wear tomorrow. A nightgown. My lotion. But she couldn't stand the idea of strangers retrieving her belongings for her. "I'm okay."

"I'll need to get in touch with you tomorrow, Brooke."

"It's a work day." During the many traumatic twists and turns that marked the long months of her separation from Thomas and her devastating divorce, she'd always found solace in returning to her job, in keeping busy. "I'll be at the boutique."

A few minutes later, she was behind the steering wheel of her car with her backpack on the passenger seat beside her. It took some maneuvering for all the police and emergency vehicles to clear a path, but she managed to get past them. She made the tight turn onto the snow-packed road that led down the side of the cliff.

She was glad to leave it all behind her, but she couldn't relax. Her lungs were still clenched. Tension gripped the muscles in her back and neck.

The fear that she'd fought so hard to control returned to haunt her. She hated feeling like a coward—it made her feel weak and out of control.

Usually, the cool silence of the night would have soothed her. In the few months that she'd been in Colorado, she'd reveled in peaceful solitude.

But that was before danger had found her. The tension inside her built. Her gloved fingers tightened on the steering wheel. She couldn't get the image of Sally out of her mind. "It's wrong. So wrong," she muttered.

She pulled up at the stop sign at the bottom of the hill. She needed to vent—to express her fear and, in so doing, loosen its hold.

Keeping her hands on the steering wheel, she yelled in protest. It was a battle cry—loud and guttural, wrenched from deep inside her. Then she yelled again. Screaming in the car was something that psychos did, but she had to let it out, had to find release in her fight against the invisible demon of fear. "I am a good person. I deserve a normal, quiet life. Is that too much to ask? Is it?"

The night answered her with overwhelming silence. For a moment, her fear seemed almost insignificant as she looked through the windshield at the massive mountains and the moonlight glistening on the snow. The pine trees watched like sentinels.

Her breath began to come more easily.

Turning left, she drove cautiously on the curving road that bordered Squirrel Creek as she considered the practical problem of where to stay tonight. During ski season, even the cheapest accommodations in Aspen were too expensive for her budget, and just about every place was fully booked anyway. She glanced down to check her gas gauge. She had enough to drive to Glenwood Springs, where it was likely she'd find an affordable place to stay.

She actually didn't want to be in Aspen. The last thing she needed was to run into someone she knew—or worse, someone who knew Sally. Though Aspen was a world-class resort, there was a small-town feeling among the local merchants, hotel staff and those who worked in the ski industry. Everybody was into everybody else's business.

She turned left onto the shortcut to Glenwood, a two-lane road with snow piled up on both sides. The clock on her dashboard showed that it was after ten o'clock. Most people were either home in bed or propped up on a bar stool in their favorite tavern.

Headlights in her rearview mirror caught her attention. They seemed to be approaching too fast. The bright high beams came closer. Like two shining eyes, glaring.

The muscles in her leg tightened as she pressed down on the accelerator. In seconds, the speedometer read fifty-five, which wasn't an unreasonable speed for this straight road across an open meadow—unless she hit an icy patch.

The vehicle behind her matched her pace, staying a few lengths behind. Her gaze flicked to the rearview mirror, then back to the road ahead. There were no houses close to the road. No ready escape.

Her usually reliable Jeep station wagon jostled and jolted. She felt a clunk. A fierce vibration rattled the frame.

A flat tire.

The steering wheel jerked in her hands. She had to slow down. There was no other choice.

She wanted to believe that the driver of that truck meant her no harm, that the hate-filled face she'd seen at the house was only an illusion, that Michael's story about a serial killer was crazy.

But if she was wrong…she was a dead woman.

Chapter Three

Breathing hard, Brooke pulled over at a wide spot in the road, parking next to a pile of snow left behind by the plow. Dread crashed over her. Panic came roaring back with the force of an avalanche.

She watched as the truck that had been behind her swept past. Just that quickly, the other vehicle was gone.

The truck hadn't been following her. She was safe. Throwing off her seat belt, she took a deep breath and waited for the panic to subside. Now all she had to do was deal with a flat, find a place to stay and hang on to her sanity.

The shortcut to Glenwood Springs wasn't exactly the middle of nowhere—but close enough. The nearest house lights appeared to be at least a mile away. She could hike there, but she hesitated to leave the safety of her car. Walking through the night, she'd be vulnerable.

Another set of headlights shone through the windshield. Was he coming back? She squinted through the night. The lights were too low to be a truck. It was a different vehicle, maybe someone who could help her. People who lived in the mountains tended to be understanding about car problems. She might be able to flag them down.

The headlights came closer. Her fingers closed around the door handle. If she jumped out and waved, the other car would surely stop. *Ask for help. Get yourself out of this mess.*

She withdrew her hand, unwilling to play the role of a helpless Southern belle. In her experience, it wasn't smart to depend on the kindness of strangers.

The car zoomed past without slowing.

Being alone was good. She could take care of herself. She could change the tire…or at least call someone who could. Handling the situation by herself would help her reclaim control of her life. A false claim, for sure. She had no control. Zero.

She pounded her fist on the steering wheel. Her house was a crime scene. Her roommate was dead. And she was the target of a serial killer. No reason to fall apart, right? *Be rational. Focus on the present.*

Her first consideration was the flat tire. She'd bought these tires only a few weeks ago because they were guaranteed to do well in snow, and she'd been driving on them long enough that she didn't think they were defective. How had she gotten a flat? Had someone sabotaged her tire?

Another car approached. Instead of passing, it slowed and parked behind her. Coming to help? Or coming to hurt her?

Frantically, she cranked the ignition. Even if it meant driving on the rim, she had to escape.

Someone tapped on the glass. She looked up and saw Michael outside her window. "Let's go, Brooke."

She didn't want *his* help. She rolled down her window. "I have a flat."

His hand rested on the butt of his gun as he stared down

the road. Then he leaned down to her level. "Somebody disabled your vehicle. They wanted you stranded. Get out of the car, and come with me."

Only seconds ago, she'd considered the same conclusion. Her flat tire wasn't a coincidence. Neither was the fact that Michael was here. "Did you follow me?"

"Damn right."

She hated to have him hovering around like some sort of aggravating guardian angel, but it would be silly not to take advantage of his presence. She opened the car door and grabbed her backpack. "I'd appreciate a ride into town. I can get one of the guys from the gas station to come fix the flat."

"Sure." He grasped her arm and guided her toward his sedan.

"I can walk on my own, Michael."

"Then you'd best walk fast," he said. "No point in standing here like a target."

"No point at all," she agreed.

She ran to the passenger side of his SUV and climbed inside. Michael hit the gas, and they zoomed away. He kept checking his mirrors, alert to any approaching threat.

In spite of the snow and icy spots, they shot down the road, fast but controlled. She liked the way he drove, his hands strong and confident on the wheel. With satisfaction, she noticed that he was wearing the black leather gloves he'd bought on her recommendation. Like everything in the boutique, the gloves were very expensive, and she'd been a bit surprised that a cop from Birmingham could afford the exorbitant price.

"My best guess," he said, "is that the killer punched a hole in your tire, causing a slow leak."

"When could he have done that?"

"Right after you arrived at your house. Or maybe he waited until later and shot a bullet into the tire. There was a lot of confusion."

"I didn't hear gunfire."

"Silencer," he said. "He could have done it when you pulled up at the stop sign. You sat there for a good, long while. I could see your tail lights when I was trying to get out of the driveway."

Though he was talking about a serial killer with a gun, she felt the band of tension squeezing her lungs begin to loosen. Breathing came more easily. In the warm interior of his car, she relaxed. The questions she should have been asking about why he'd come after her and what he wanted from her seemed unimportant. For the moment, she felt safe.

He stopped at an intersection. No headlights were visible in any direction. "I think we're good," he said, looking in the rearview mirror.

She gazed at him, taking in his high forehead, deep-set eyes and firm jaw. He had that deceptively lazy look that she thought of as Southern and sultry.

She leaned back against the seat, aware of the bone-deep weariness that came in the aftermath of danger. What she needed right now was to sleep, to curl up in a ball and go completely unconscious. But there was more to do tonight, and she needed to get organized. "If you take a right here and drive for a couple of miles to Lander's Crossing, then another right, we'll be headed back toward Aspen."

"Got it." He drove for a moment in silence, then he said, "We need to talk about a few things, Brooke."

She held up her hand, forestalling any more warnings. "Not about your serial killer. I've had enough for today."

"You need to know what to expect. I'm not just whistling Dixie. This killer is real."

"Then why didn't the FBI contact me?"

"Good question. And I have a real good explanation," he drawled. "It all started about a month ago, at the end of October. I got word from Atlanta that Grant Rawlins had been killed. It was an execution-style murder with one bullet through the forehead and another in his heart."

Grant Rawlins. His name brought back memories of the trial. Locked up in a bland room in the Atlanta courthouse, their deliberations lasted a whole day. She remembered being tired, watching the afternoon sun pouring through the windows and fading to dusk, knowing that they would have to return the next day to finalize their verdict.

At that time, three years ago, her marriage had already sprung a leak. Thomas had been with another woman, but he'd broken off the affair. She'd forgiven him, confident that they could get their marriage back on course. His career was beginning to take off, and she'd been proud to be his wife.

Back then she'd been a solidly married woman who would never dream of being unfaithful. Still, she couldn't help noticing Grant Rawlins—a dark, handsome man with a subtle charisma. He moved athletically in spite of his prosthetic leg. "We elected Grant to be foreman of the jury."

"He was a leader," Michael said proudly. "We served together in the Marines."

"He told me he lost his leg in the service," she said.

"And saved my life." His jaw tensed. "Grant was a true hero. And I want justice for his murder."

She shifted uncomfortably, not wanting to continue the discussion but intrigued by Michael's story. "Surely there was an investigation."

"The Atlanta PD did a decent job. They were the ones who made the link to the jury that convicted Robby Lee Warren. When he got killed in prison, there were plenty of people screaming for revenge. Robby Lee's three brothers. His father. And the thugs he ran with."

"But nobody was arrested for Grant's murder?"

"Not enough evidence. Too many alibis." He took the turn that lead toward Aspen. "The case went cold, but I couldn't put the murder behind me. I kept seeing Grant, lying in his coffin with his Purple Heart ribbon pinned to his lapel. So I took a six-month leave of absence from my job to focus all my efforts on finding his killer."

Michael's loyalty was fierce—she understood his need to solve this crime. "You said there were other deaths."

"Juror number two died in what looked like a car accident. I tried to make the case that Grant's murderer had set up the accident, but the two murders were so different that they didn't fit FBI profiles."

"And the third juror?"

"Disappeared. The body hasn't been found." He gave her a long look. "That's why I'm here with you. I owe it to Grant to keep you safe."

Her typical I-can-take-care-of-myself response stuck in her craw. She couldn't easily dismiss his story, turn her back and walk away. His logic made sense. And his emotional response to his friend's death rang true.

She believed him.

Accepting Michael's story affected her in ways that couldn't be ignored. Ever since she moved to Aspen, she'd been recuperating from her horror-story divorce. The mountains had healed her. She thought she was recovered, but his words awakened her fears. It felt like she'd gone to the doctor with a headache and found out that she had a fatal illness. Michael had pronounced her death sentence.

She had a terrible thought that she didn't want to put into words. But she had to. "Did he kill my roommate thinking that she was me?"

"I don't know your roommate, but it sounds like she had other people who might want her dead. And I suppose we should still consider the possibility that she committed suicide."

"Give me an answer, Michael."

"I can't say for sure."

"I need to know if she died in my place." How could Brooke ever forgive herself? Her eyes burned, and she squeezed them shut, fighting the tears.

"I'm sorry," he said.

"Me, too."

MICHAEL HADN'T wanted to make her feel guilty for her roommate's death. If anyone was to blame, it was him. He'd known about the threat and hadn't moved quickly enough. That wasn't a mistake he'd make a second time. "Where were you headed tonight?"

"Glenwood Springs."

"Why so far away?"

"My budget. Glenwood is less expensive. And I wanted to get away from all this. From Sally's death." Her voice began to quaver. "But I can't get away. Not when I could be responsible for her death. I can't run fast enough or far enough to hide from the guilt."

Covering her face with her hands, she leaned forward. Her long hair tumbled around her face. Her shoulders shook convulsively as she wept.

He pulled into a parking lot outside a convenience store

on the outskirts of town. Slipping the car into Park, he kept the engine running and the heater cranked on High. Though it wasn't snowing, these mountains were freezing cold.

Tentatively, he reached toward her. After all these years as a cop, he still didn't know how to handle a woman who was crying. He liked it better when Brooke was snarling at him, brandishing a butcher knife. At least he knew how to handle that. Her tears made him feel helpless.

When he touched her shoulder, she pulled away—a standard reaction from a woman who had been abused. From Brooke's records, he knew that she was divorced and had taken out a restraining order against her ex-husband. He suspected there was a lot more to that story.

She turned her tear-stained face toward him. "I'm okay. We can go."

"If you'd like," he said, "I could go get you some water. Or coffee."

"I'm all right."

She swiped the back of her hand across her cheek, leaving smudges of mascara under her bright blue eyes. Her nose was red, and her full lips pinched together to hold back more sobs. Bedraggled and exhausted, she was a mess. His mama would have said that Brooke looked like something the cat dragged in. And yet, he couldn't take his eyes off this beautiful, vulnerable woman. Her pain and sorrow were raw, honest.

"You're staying with me tonight," he said. "In my hotel room. I'll sleep on the sofa, and you can take the bed."

"I don't think so." She tossed her head, sending ripples through her auburn hair. "I lost control for a moment, but I haven't lost my mind."

"This topic isn't up for discussion. The only way I'll know you're safe is if I can keep an eye on you."

"What about my car?"

"I'll take care of it. The only thing you need to worry about is getting some sleep."

As he drove into Aspen, he listened with half an ear while she told him she was capable of taking care of herself and certainly didn't need him hanging around like some kind of cut-rate bodyguard. She wanted to be alone, needing solitude to regroup.

But finally she admitted her exhaustion. "Maybe it wouldn't hurt to stay with you for one night. It's not like this is a date or anything."

"Far from it."

The fact that she is a beautiful and desirable woman doesn't matter a whit. My mission is to keep her alive. No one else would die at the hand of Robby Lee Warren's avenger. In that way, Michael would honor the vow he'd made to the memory of Grant Rawlins.

At the hotel, he turned his car keys over to the valet while Brooke looked at him with a curious expression.

"Nice hotel," she said.

"I thought so."

"At the boutique this afternoon, you didn't wince when I told you how much those gorgeous leather gloves cost."

He nodded.

"There aren't many cops who can afford the prices in Aspen."

"I suppose Aspen is a bit pricey." He glanced at the streets of the mountain town, decorated with garlands and sparkling lights. "Reminds me of a Christmas card."

"Classy but quaint," she said. "When I lived in Atlanta, I always missed the snow at Christmastime."

"I could do without the cold."

At the door to the hotel, a young man in jeans and a ski patrol parka called out, "Brooke! Hey, Brooke!"

She held up a hand to acknowledge the guy, but she clearly didn't want to talk to him.

He hustled closer—close enough that Michael could smell the beer on his breath when he said, "I heard about what happened to Sally."

Brooke edged closer to Michael. "There was nothing I could do."

"It was suicide, right?"

"I don't know."

"I never knew anybody who killed themselves. Amazing." He dragged his fingers through his shaggy brown hair. In spite of the mountain cold, he wasn't wearing gloves or a hat. "Wait until Tyler hears about this."

Tyler who? Michael had to wonder. Despite his conviction that Sally had been mistakenly killed by the serial killer, further investigation might be necessary.

In a glance, he analyzed the man who stood before him—a typical tanned ski bum, carefree and full of beer. But he had an edge, an anger in the depths of his brown eyes. Michael held out his hand and introduced himself.

After a muscular handshake, the young man said, "I'm Peter Thorne."

"And you were friends with Sally," Michael said.

"Hell, I slept with her."

Beside him, he heard Brooke inhale a sharp gasp. "That's enough, Peter."

"I might have been her first score when she got to Aspen," he said. "Didn't take Sally long to move on to bigger fish, though. Guys who were famous and rich, like Tyler Hennessey."

"Never heard of him," Michael said.

"Man, you are definitely not from Aspen. Tyler's a superstar. For sure, he'll be going to the Olympics in snowboarding."

Michael barely knew what snowboarding was. "So, Sally dumped you for this superstar?"

He gave a hard laugh. "Dropped me like a landslide."

Though Michael's first concern was to get Brooke safely to the room, he wanted to find out more from Peter Thorne. "Breaking up is no fun. That must have ticked you off."

"I'll tell you this." He jabbed a drunken forefinger toward Michael's chest. "Sally ticked off a lot of people. Am I right, Brooke?"

Silently, she nodded.

"I wouldn't be surprised," said Peter, "if this wasn't a suicide. There are lots of guys who wouldn't mind seeing Sally Klinger dead."

"We have to go," Brooke said. "Good night, Peter."

Michael watched Peter stagger along the sidewalk. There seemed to be no lack of motive for people who wanted to hurt Brooke's roommate. Boyfriends. Ex-boyfriends. Her husband.

Even Brooke had admitted that she wanted to get Sally out of her life.

He took another look at the auburn-haired beauty who entered the hotel in front of him. Had her anger toward her roommate turned violent? Was it possible that the woman he'd come to protect from a serial killer was a murderer?

Chapter Four

With Brooke asleep in the bedroom in his hotel suite, Michael poured himself a shot of Kentucky bourbon and added ice—a sin to purists, but he liked his liquor cold.

After Grant's murder, he'd gotten into the habit of having a drink every night before he went to bed in the hope that he wouldn't lie awake, unable to shut off his mind. The fact that Grant's killer hadn't been brought to justice tore him up inside.

For ten years, Michael had been chasing down leads and solving crimes, but his experience as a cop was no help at all when it came to dealing with Grant's murder. He raised his glass to the memory of his friend. *Here's to a fallen comrade. A good man, a good soldier, a good friend. Semper Fi.*

The bourbon rolled across his tongue, leaving a mellow aftertaste. The hotel's concierge had stocked the kitchenette with the things he'd requested: milk, fruit and bourbon. Two healthy items out of three wasn't bad.

The hotel was turning out to be more than adequate. The spacious living room with a view of the ski slope had a kitchenette and a small bathroom of its own. In spite of the earthy Southwestern colors, the rustic furniture reminded him of his uncle Elmo's hunting lodge. Although the hunting lodge had just about as much class as a rusted tin can.

He listened but heard no sound from the bedroom. Within minutes after Brooke said good-night and closed the bedroom door, he heard her running the shower in the bathroom. If his prior experience with victims held true, he figured she'd be scrubbing herself clean, trying to wash away the memory of violence.

But was she a victim? He gave serious consideration to the possibility that Brooke might have killed her roommate. It seemed unlikely that Brooke had the necessary physical strength to haul Sally through the house and fling her over the balcony. Also, when he arrived on the scene, Brooke's desperation was real—she wanted to help Sally, to save her.

Nope, Brooke wasn't a killer.

He had the sense that she was stressed to her breaking point, though. It seemed that her life had been a rough ride, and one more bump in the road—finding her roommate dead—could send her over the edge. Sally's death wasn't just a bump in the road—it was more like getting mowed down by a trauma the size of a semi-truck.

Crossing the room, he turned on the gas fireplace and sat on the sofa. His laptop rested on the coffee table in front of him. Time to review his research on the lady who had taken over his bedroom. Thirty-two years old. No arrests. No criminal record. She'd been secretary of the Atlanta Junior League. Active in charity events, her picture popped up on the society page. The black-and-white photo showed a slender, unsmiling woman standing beside an athletic-looking guy in a tux. Her husband, Thomas. She'd taken out a restraining order on him and filed two police reports

claiming that he'd harassed her. After a prolonged separation and court battle, their divorce was final four months
ago. She'd left town almost immediately afterward.

What made this lady tick? She'd readily admitted that
she sometimes saw things that weren't there but wasn't
currently on medications. Very likely she'd been seeing a
therapist. It sure would be handy to talk to that counselor,
but psychiatrists wouldn't talk without a warrant—and
sometimes not even then.

First thing tomorrow, he'd put in a call to a friend in the
Atlanta police department and see if he could unearth any
pertinent information on Brooke Johnson.

Stripped down to his shorts, he pulled the sofa into a
bed and got between the sheets. He closed his eyes and
relaxed into unconsciousness.

HIS DREAM state didn't last all night. A sound from behind
the bedroom door pulled him awake. Immediately, he was
out of bed and on his feet. The digital clock in the kitchen
showed the time: it was 1:07 a.m. Poised for action, he
listened hard. The sound came again—a small whimper.
He wasn't surprised that this subtle noise woke him. Ever
since serving in a combat zone, he'd been a light sleeper.

What was going on in that bedroom? It didn't seem
possible that an intruder had broken in. They were on the
third floor, and there was no access through the windows.
All the same, he needed to check on Brooke's safety.

Gun in hand, he eased the bedroom door open. Moonlight poured through the window.

He saw her curled up in a tight ball with the covers
thrown aside. Her shoulders trembled, and he realized that
she had made the noise. It was a quiet sob that tore at his
heart. She uncoiled and rolled over, her head thrashing

back and forth in denial. Her eyes were closed—she was still asleep and dreaming of her own private sorrows.

He approached the bed and placed his gun on the night-stand. Standing over her, he couldn't help but admire her long, slender legs and slim torso. Her dark red hair—the rich color of cherry wood—tangled around her face. Her full lips moved, but no words came out.

Careful not to disturb her, he pulled the comforter back over her. Very gently, he smoothed the hair off her face.

A long, low groan pushed through her lips. She seemed to relax; her breath came more easily. In the moonlight, her skin was luminescent. Her delicate features shone with a natural beauty that was a wonder to behold.

But he couldn't allow himself to be attracted to her. He hadn't come all the way across the country to find a lover. Taking his gun from the table, he left her bedroom and returned to the sofa bed.

Less than an hour later, she cried out again. This time, it was a loud shout.

Michael bolted from sleep and ran to her bedroom. He found her cowering in the corner beside the open drapes, as if she was trying to protect herself from a beating.

When she saw him, she stood up straight. Her body was stiff; tension radiated from every pore. In a shaky voice, she asked, "Where am I?"

"In a hotel in Aspen."

His words seemed to confuse her. She shook her head. Her hands clenched into two fists, and she raised them to her mouth. "Who are you?"

"Michael Shaw," he said as gently as possible. "I'm not going to hurt you, Brooke."

Her gaze focused on the gun he held in his hand. "Leave me alone. Please. Please."

"You're safe, Brooke." He set the gun down on the dresser. "I'm here to protect you. You can go back to bed. Nothing's going to hurt you."

Stiffly, she edged along the wall until she reached the bed. Her movements were clumsy as she got under the covers. "You can go. I'm fine."

"Are you sure about that?"

"Go," she said. "Please. Go away."

He wasn't sure that she was awake. Not fully conscious, anyway. Caught up in her nightmare, she'd lost track of the present, hurtling backward in time to relive a bad experience. Her behavior reminded him of combat veterans with post-traumatic stress disorder.

Though she hadn't been to war, some parts of her life must have felt like a battlefield. That ex-husband of hers had really done a number on her.

THE NEXT morning, Brooke sat across the table from Michael, eating the breakfast he'd ordered from room service. Waffles for him. Eggs Benedict for her. She'd already taken a shower and washed her hair. All in all, she felt okay in spite of her nightmares and the nagging half memory that she'd done something embarrassing last night, like sleepwalking.

She poured herself a cup of coffee and added her usual three packets of sugar. Her own version of extra sweet tasted better to her than any of the fancy concoctions from the coffee specialty shops.

Her first bite of egg was excellent. The second even better. She dug in, glad to be hungry. She'd need all her strength to get through today.

"I usually don't eat so much breakfast," she said.

"My aunt Hester used to say it was the most important meal of the day."

"Aunt Hester, huh? She sounds like something out of an antebellum novel."

"She was real. A true Southern belle."

His voice struck exactly the right tone of friendliness, but there was something in his eyes that worried her. He seemed to be taking her measure, deciding how he ought to handle her.

And she was also wary—unsure if she wanted his help but afraid to be on her own. If there truly was a serial killer after her, she could do a lot worse than having this handsome cop from Birmingham as a protector.

"I want to thank you," she said, "for letting me stay here last night."

"No problem." He took a huge bite of waffle, drizzled with syrup and butter. "I'm glad you didn't have to drive all the way across the mountain to Glenwood Springs."

"So am I."

Her decision to drive toward Glenwood Springs hadn't been entirely logical, but she had wanted to put distance between herself and the place where Sally died. Her instinct had been to run—to escape the inevitable gossip and avoid the questions.

She knew what it was like to be at the center of a terrible situation. When her marriage exploded, she'd faced constant, cruel, judgmental scrutiny. Though Atlanta ranked as one of the largest cities in the South, her shame made the streets shrink to a microcosm. Everywhere she went—to her job, to the grocery store, to the gym—she encountered people who knew her and Thomas. Some looked upon her with pity. Others regarded her with disgust, unable to understand how she could leave her very influential, very handsome husband. How dare she take out a restraining order against him? Clearly she was a crazy, ungrateful witch.

They couldn't know what happened inside their marriage, and she was too proud to tell the truth. No woman wants to admit that she allowed herself to be trapped in an abusive relationship. She should have left Thomas much sooner than she did.

She attacked her eggs with renewed vigor.

"You'll be staying here again tonight," he said.

"That won't be necessary. I'm sure the police will be done with my house."

"Even so, you'll need to have the locks changed. And I'll be hiring a cleaning service to put things back in order."

He was right about the locks. "I can't let you pay for a cleaning service. After I get my car fixed, I can—"

"Already taken care of," he said. "I made a phone call last night. Your tire is repaired, and your car is parked in the hotel garage."

She should have been grateful, but there was something unnerving about having him step in and run her life. She needed to set some boundaries. Laying her fork down on her plate, she confronted him directly. "I insist on paying for the repair. How much do I owe you?"

"Money isn't a problem."

It hadn't escaped her notice that this was a very deluxe suite in a hotel that wasn't cheap. The classic Southwestern style was gorgeous. And the master bathroom had a Jacuzzi, polished granite countertops and pewter fixtures. From the little she knew about his background, she didn't expect him to be wealthy. "Do you mind if I ask why?"

He looked up from the waffle, which was rapidly disappearing. "Why what?"

"Why isn't money a problem?"

Avoiding her gaze, he refilled his coffee cup. No sugar for him. "Family inheritance."

His terse response made her think he was uncomfortable talking about himself. His reticence made her even more curious, of course. "When I think of Birmingham, I think steel. Was that the business your family was in?"

"Steel and manufacturing. Then we moved into farming. My sister runs the business, and she's branched into biotech research, which has turned out to be profitable and just might save the world."

"And you have a share in this family business?"

"I'm on the board of directors."

That explained why he had money but said very little about Michael himself. "You could have been a gentleman farmer, but you went into the Marines?"

"Signing up for military service is something that every male in the Shaw family has done for generations. It's tradition."

"Afterward, why did you become a cop?"

He sipped his coffee and shrugged his broad shoulders. The forest green of his crewneck sweater almost matched the color of his eyes. "My sister and my mama have asked me that very question about ten million times. I don't have a real good answer."

"I'd like to know," she said. "Since we're going to be spending some time together, it would help if I understood a little bit about you."

"Same here." He leaned forward. "I'd like to know about you, Brooke."

Exploring her past was a perilous journey, but she had plenty of practice in saying just enough. "You first. Why are you a cop?"

"My time in the Marines got cut short. I was given a medical discharge after I had a pretty severe head injury.

I was in a coma for a week. It happened in the same incident that cost Grant Rawlins his leg."

"I'm sorry," she said. "Are you all right?"

"Mostly. I have occasional vertigo."

To her eyes, he appeared to be in peak physical condition. She had a sudden image of Michael wearing only black boxer shorts. She saw sinewy arms, muscular thighs and a gun in his hand. She blinked to erase that thought, concentrating one hundred percent on the remains of her breakfast. "Please continue."

"When I left the Corps, it didn't seem like I'd completed my mission. In war zones, I saw a lot of injustice. Cruelty. Pain. I'll spare you the details."

Though his expression didn't change, she sensed his tension as he continued. "I was left with the feeling that I needed to do what I could to make things right. Being a cop seemed like a good fit. To serve and protect."

His sincerity and idealism lifted him in her estimation. He was a rich man who could have coasted through life. Instead, he truly wanted to help others. "That's very impressive."

"Now it's my turn," he said. "I have a few questions for you, starting with—"

"Wait." She glanced at her clock. "I'm afraid that discussion will have to wait. I'm supposed to open the shop today, and I need to be there by nine thirty."

"You're putting me off," he said. It was a statement, not a question; clearly he recognized her avoidance tactic. "If you don't tell me about yourself, I'll have to rely on what other people say about you."

What other people? She brushed his comment away. "We'll talk about me later. I promise."

"That's fine," he said in an exaggerated drawl that made

two words sound like ten. "Before we leave this room, we need to lay down some ground rules."

She didn't like the sound of this. "Such as?"

"Until I learn otherwise, I'm going to assume that you're in danger. Don't go anywhere by yourself."

"What about work?"

"I'll go with you to the shop. You can open up. Then you can call somebody to fill in for you." He finished off the last bite of waffle and dropped his napkin on the plate. "I'm sure your employer will understand if you take a couple days off."

That was very likely true. Hannah Lewis was an understanding boss. But Brooke preferred working. The best way to handle a crisis was to keep busy. "I'll be safe at the boutique. Nobody is going to attack me with other people standing around."

"I was in your little shop yesterday," he reminded her. "It's not exactly a hotbed of activity."

"Yesterday was the Tuesday after Thanksgiving weekend. Of course, it was slow."

"And today?"

"I'm pretty sure there will be a crowd," she said. "Everybody is going to be stopping by, wanting to know the details about Sally's death. Aspen isn't Birmingham. This is a small community. People will be curious."

"Nonetheless, you need to make arrangements for later this morning," he said. "At eleven o'clock, you need to report to McGraw's office. I'll be there, too. I have an appointment to talk to the feds."

"The FBI?" Though she wanted to deny that she was the next target of a serial killer, a shiver trickled down her spine.

He crossed the room to the coffee table and picked up

his laptop. After punching a few keys, he turned the screen toward her. "This is Robby Lee Warren's oldest brother. His name is Stonewall Jackson Warren. He goes by Jackson."

"Robert E. Lee and Stonewall Jackson?"

"The other brothers are Jefferson Davis and John Morgan. All generals in the Confederate Army."

"Should I be asking if all your relatives who enlisted were fighting for the South?"

"Probably not," he said.

She looked at the screen. Though Stonewall Jackson Warren was smiling in the picture, he had a piercing stare. His eyebrows arched like wings over his brown eyes. He had dark hair, a long face and prominent cheekbones. "He's not bad looking."

"Con men usually aren't," Michael said. "Jackson Warren has a history of running scams and pulling off minor frauds. He's been arrested twice but never been brought to trial."

"Why not?"

"He's cunning, always has a dodge. Though he's nothing more than a petty criminal, he's intelligent and mean. A lethal combination."

"Do you think he's the killer?"

"He's the one I'd pick."

"Then it ought to be easy to find out if he killed Sally. We can contact the Atlanta police and check his alibi."

"If they could find him," he said darkly. "The whole family has scattered like seeds in the wind. None of them have a permanent address or contact. They could be anywhere. That's why I want you to be able to recognize him."

"Because he might be here." It dawned on her that she

might have another stalker. Was this her fate? To be menaced by men wherever she went? "I hate this."

"So do I."

She looked up at him and saw determination and strength in his eyes. She realized that Michael Shaw was the difference between what had happened in Atlanta and what could happen in Aspen. He had her back. He was dedicated to protecting her.

"I'm glad you're here, Michael."

He nodded in response and looked back at the screen. "Jackson is average height, average build. Doesn't stand out in a crowd."

She concentrated on the photo. "I think I remember seeing him at Robby Lee's trial."

"Here's the rest of the clan."

As Michael scrolled through mug shots of the other brothers and father, her memory became clearer. She'd seen them all. The whole Warren family had attended the trial, supporting the baby brother.

"Remember these faces," Michael said. "These men have sworn to avenge Robby Lee's death."

Fear sank into her bones as she realized that she might be looking into the cold, dark eyes of men who wanted her dead.

Chapter Five

The sheriff's department was housed in the Pitkin County Courthouse, an impressive red stone structure that had been built in the late 1800s when Aspen was a thriving mining community. Standing on a pedestal above the front entrance was a life-size, silver statue of Lady Justice. Though she held her scales, she was without a blindfold so she could keep an eye on the town.

In the corridor outside Deputy McGraw's office, Michael sat waiting while Brooke gave her statement to the deputy and two FBI agents from Denver. Though the feds had arrived, he knew better than to set his expectations too high. Each time he'd met with the FBI, they shot down his theory, calling it improbable. If he'd been a private citizen instead of a decorated veteran and police detective, Michael had no doubt that he would have been labeled a crank and summarily ignored.

The door to McGraw's office opened, and Brooke stepped out. Shoulders back and chin held high, she looked angry. Her blue eyes flashed. "I'm going back to work," she said.

McGraw waved him in. "We're ready for you, Michael."

"I want you to wait for me," he said to her.

"I have no need for an escort," she said through pinched lips. "These gentlemen don't believe I'm in any danger."

But he did. Even if he hadn't known all the details, his instincts would have sensed a threat. "I'll be done in a minute. Sit right here."

"Fine." She perched on the edge of a chair with her back as stiff as a steel rod.

He entered the office, and McGraw closed the door behind him. The big man lumbered around the office and took a seat behind his desk. "Can I get you anything to drink, Michael?"

A stiff shot of bourbon would be mighty fine. "No, thanks."

The two FBI agents were dressed in casual slacks and sweaters for their visit to Aspen, but they were uniformly well-groomed and neat. Agent Franklin had blond hair. Agent Ramirez was dark. Both gave him unsmiling nods as he took the vacant chair on the far side of the desk, away from them and from the deputy.

In a low rumble, McGraw said, "Sally Klinger didn't commit suicide. Her death was homicide."

"What brought you to that conclusion?"

"Primarily the physical evidence," McGraw said. "We didn't find a note. The knot and the way the rope was positioned would have made it difficult for her to jump over the balcony."

"Were there indications of a struggle on the body?" Michael asked. "Premortem bruising?"

"Our coroner isn't equipped to do full autopsies, not with blood workups and DNA tests. We don't have many homicides up here." He sounded apologetic. "We've sent the body to the Denver crime labs. However, there was a bit of bruising inconsistent with suicide. And a needle mark just above her collarbone."

"It must have been difficult to spot that mark," Michael said. "I'm assuming the rope left abrasions on her throat."

"We might not be a big city crime lab," McGraw said, "but our coroner is a sharp guy. He thinks she was injected with a sedative, then strung up."

"Sounds like a killer who knew what he was doing. An organized murder." He aimed a steady gaze at the FBI agents. "This wasn't a crime of passion."

"Agreed," Ramirez said. "A profile of the evidence indicates someone who planned carefully and came to the crime scene with the intent to commit murder."

"Almost like an execution," Michael said.

"We're familiar with your theory about a serial killer," Ramirez said. "But Sally Klinger wasn't a member of the jury."

"No, but she looks enough like Brooke Johnson for the killer to have mistaken her identity. She was wearing items of Brooke's clothing. And a wristwatch inscribed to Brooke."

Ramirez leaned forward in his chair. "A killer who planned so carefully would never make such a mistake. He came to that house to kill Sally Klinger, and that's exactly what he did."

He had a point about the ID—it didn't seem like a mistake this killer would make. But Michael was still unwilling to concede. "What was the killer's motive?"

"Sally was a party girl," Ramirez said. "From an analysis of the victimology, we know that she had several boyfriends she dated and discarded. And a husband back in Denver."

"Does this husband have an alibi?"

McGraw spoke up. "He claimed to be with his girl-friend all night, and she backs him up."

"Anybody else who can verify that?"

Slowly, McGraw shook his head. "They were home alone. And we weren't able to talk to the husband until this morning, which means he had plenty of time to commit the crime here and drive back to Denver."

"That's a long trip. He must have stopped to get gas. If he didn't pay cash, there would be a record."

"We're checking that," McGraw said. "Actually, we're working with the Colorado Bureau of Investigation, and they'll be doing most of the legwork."

"Did Sally have any other family?" Though Michael wasn't technically on this case, he slipped easily into the familiar role of police detective. From experience, he knew that the likely suspects were those who benefited from the crime. "Maybe someone who'd collect on an in-surance policy?"

"We haven't got all the paperwork figured out yet, but money isn't a motive. Not for her immediate family. They're wealthy enough. Her parents and younger sister are in New Zealand for the winter. They aren't snowbirds like Sally."

"That leaves only the boyfriends."

"Or someone else who hated Sally," Ramirez said.

Though he didn't actually name Brooke, the implica-tion was clear. Brooke had readily admitted to Michael that she didn't like her roommate and wanted her gone. For a moment, even he had suspected her. But that was only a fleeting thought—and a foolish one at that.

These feds were beginning to annoy him, and when he got annoyed, he reverted to his Southern-gentleman roots. In an exaggerated drawl, he asked, "Did y'all happen to have anyone particular in mind?"

"Sally was an abrasive personality. Hard to get along with," Ramirez said. "I'm willing to bet she had as many enemies as friends."

A vague statement that didn't tell him anything about their suspicions. "The killer couldn't have been a woman. A female wouldn't have the physical strength to stage that hanging."

"Depends on the female," Ramirez said. "All those boyfriends must have had girlfriends who hated Sally."

Michael didn't buy this scenario. "A female killer is highly unlikely."

Ramirez frowned. Apparently, he didn't like being contradicted. "A woman could have hired a professional assassin to make it look like a suicide."

"A pro wouldn't have neglected to leave a note," Michael pointed out. "I remember a laptop in her bedroom. Was there a note on the computer?"

"We didn't find anything," McGraw said as he closed the folder on his desk and pushed it away from him. The gesture seemed to indicate that he was ready to be done with this conversation. "It's possible that Brooke interrupted the killer before he could completely set the crime scene."

If they were still suspicious of Brooke, they hadn't zeroed in on her as the primary suspect. He was relieved. After last night, his instinct to protect Brooke was on overdrive. If anything, she was a victim. A survivor of trauma. *Not a killer.*

"It's too darn bad that Brooke can't give us a better description. She saw the guy," McGraw said.

"Allegedly," Ramirez said.

For the first time, his partner, Agent Franklin, spoke up.

"She wasn't sure that she actually saw anyone. She admitted to us that her mind might have been playing tricks on her. Brooke was in a hyperdelusional state, behaving irrationally, stalking through her house with an ax."

"She meant to use the ax to cut the rope," Michael countered. "When I found her, she was thinking that Sally was still alive and in need of CPR."

Franklin raised an eyebrow. "I believe she threatened you with a butcher knife. You found it necessary to disarm her."

He made it sound like Brooke had attacked him. "I never felt that she was truly dangerous."

"Not to you. You're a trained officer." He exchanged a glance with Ramirez. "Someone like Sally might feel differently."

Michael hated the direction this conversation was taking. Not only was it ridiculous to suspect Brooke, but these allegations pointed them even farther away from Jackson Warren.

Ramirez picked up the thread laid down by his partner. "There was no physical indication of an intruder. Nobody saw his vehicle. There were no discernible footprints."

"We can't trust Brooke's word," Franklin said. "She has a history of paranoia and delusions. In Atlanta, she made her ex-husband's life a living hell with her accusations that he was a stalker."

Michael was tempted to argue but opted to keep his mouth shut. Earlier this morning, he'd spoken to his contact on the Atlanta police force who expressed the opinion that Brooke's complaints against her ex had gone way over the top. In spite of it all, her ex-husband had been quick to move on; he'd already gotten engaged to another woman.

Michael decided he was done here—if they weren't going to help him, there was nothing more to talk about. "Bottom line—do you intend to investigate the connection between this case and the murders of the three jurors?"

"Let's be clear about this," Franklin said. "Only one was a murder. The other two were an accident and a disappearance."

"You don't believe there's a serial killer."

"My expertise is psychological profiling. A serial killer doesn't employ a diverse methodology. He likes to leave his signature at the scene."

Unless he doesn't actually want the murders to be connected. Unless he is clever enough to fool the FBI.

BROOKE HAD left the courthouse the second Deputy McGraw closed the door. She'd known that Michael would be annoyed, but she was too furious to sit docilely after the psychological thrashing she'd undergone.

Tromping down the wide front stairs that were swept clean of snow, she'd considered the possibility that she was in danger. Although the FBI certainly didn't think so. Those two agents from Denver had made it quite clear that she was, at best, a crazy paranoid. At worst, she was a suspect.

Standing on the sidewalk, she looked to the left where the Silver Queen gondola carried skiers and snowboarders up the mountain. It was gorgeous weather—made-to-order for winter sports. All the slopes accessed by the gondola were black diamond for experts only. Maybe by the end of the ski season, she'd be confident enough to try those runs. If she lived that long…

She scanned the street. The photographs of Jackson Warren and his family stayed at the forefront of her mind.

She'd recognize those faces in a heartbeat. If she saw them or anything else out of the ordinary, she'd fly back to the courthouse.

She charged down the sidewalk, heading to the safe haven of the boutique. She strode at a quick pace, trying to work off that familiar anger of not being taken seriously by authorities. Agent Ramirez and Agent Franklin wasted no time in suggesting that she had a couple of screws loose. With their smug smirks and pointed questions, they jabbed at her past, hinting that they could get a warrant to access her therapist's records and accusing her of harassing her ex-husband by taking out unnecessary restraining orders. They had her pegged as someone who desperately wanted to be in the spotlight and would do anything to get attention.

Nothing could be more inaccurate. Her idea of paradise included total anonymity. That was why she'd moved so far away from Atlanta.

Scowling, she rushed across the square. Most of the time, she enjoyed the stroll through Aspen's streets where rustic charm melded gracefully into sleek, modern condos, where a clear blue sky above the slopes held the promise of a better day. But Brooke wasn't in the mood to appreciate any of that. The dirty snow piled up at the edge of the road was a better reflection of how she felt than the flawless sky.

She spotted the sign for the boutique: Hannah's Custom Accessories. The display in the front window featured a red-and-green Christmas pyramid of leather purses and belts with sparking silver and gold jewelry. Brooke whipped open the door and leaned against it. These familiar surroundings were a sanctuary. The owner, Hannah Lewis, stood behind the counter, folding handwoven scarves and chatting with two blond women whose names Brooke couldn't remember. They looked at her with sympathy.

The taller one said, "I was so sorry to hear about Sally."

The other piped up, "Hannah said you found her body."

"There was nothing I could do," Brooke said. She'd repeated this statement a dozen times to other people who'd stopped by this morning. It was getting old. "She was dead when I got home."

"Sally sure didn't seem like the kind of person who'd kill herself. She could drink all night and go for a hike at dawn."

In measured tones, Brooke said, "Sally was a free spirit."

"Will there be a funeral? Will she be buried here?"

"I don't know."

"We should have a memorial service or something."

"Excuse me, please." Brooke brushed past them and went behind the counter to the back room. She dropped her backpack to the floor and took off her jacket, reaching up to hang it on a peg. The simple action seemed difficult. Her arms dropped to her sides, suddenly heavy and useless.

She leaned her forehead against the wall by the back door, exhausted. She squeezed her eyes shut. Once she got through today, things would start to settle down. Curiosity would fade. Tomorrow would be better.

As if from far away, she heard the two women leaving.

Hannah came into the back room. "Are you all right, honey?"

"I'm just tired." She turned to face the small, gray-haired woman in a black turtleneck and jeans with an authentic silver concha belt. Hannah always wore the same basic outfit with different accessories from the stock in the store. Today, she'd knotted a red and green scarf at her throat. Hannah always managed to look sophisticated.

"How did it go at the sheriff's office?"

Brooke tried to disguise her irritation. "I told my story again and again. No matter how many times, it still doesn't seem real. And they still seem to think I'm not telling them something."

Hannah patted her cheek. Her eyes were warm and her smile genuine. "Listen, honey. If you need to take some time off, it's okay with me."

"I'm fine."

"Really," Hannah said. "I owe you for working on Thanksgiving."

Not as much as Brooke owed Hannah for welcoming her into her home for the holiday after she closed the boutique. With Hannah's nieces and nephews visiting, her house felt wonderfully full and joyous. And the leftover turkey was delicious.

Brooke forced a smile. "I'd rather get this over with. Sally had a lot of friends, and they all want to know what happened."

"No kidding. We've had more traffic through the store this morning than we usually have in a week." She gave an ironic shrug. "If half of this crowd made purchases, we'd have a superprofitable Christmas season."

"Maybe we should run a special."

"Honey, this is Aspen. We don't do specials."

Brooke almost laughed. It was the first time since she'd found Sally's body that she'd felt anything akin to amusement.

"That's better," Hannah said. "You keep that grin on your face."

"I'll try."

With a wink, she turned her attention to a cardboard box with water stains on both sides. "I need to get these hemp purses unpacked to make sure they didn't get wet in shipping. I swear, when this stuff gets damp, it stinks like marijuana."

This time, Brooke did laugh. "Has anyone ever told you that you have a great sense of humor?"

"When you get to be my age—" a number that, to Brooke's knowledge, had never been revealed to anyone "—you'll know that laughter is the key to survival. Never take anything too seriously, and you'll be fine."

The bell over the front door jingled, and Brooke straightened her shoulders. "I'll handle this customer."

When she stepped up to the counter, she recognized Sally's latest boyfriend, Tyler Hennessey. While she struggled to find the right words of condolence, he strode to the counter. He slammed both palms on the glass and leaned toward her. His streaked blond hair fell forward, almost obscuring his eyes. His mouth curled in a snarl. "Bitch."

She took a step back. "Excuse me?"

"Is this how you get your kicks? Telling lies about me?"

"I don't know what you're talking about."

Hannah poked her head around the corner. "What's going on out here?"

"This bitch is telling everybody that I killed Sally." He slammed his palms down again. The display case shuddered. "Lies. I cared about Sally."

In spite of the barrier between them, he lunged. She saw his huge hands coming toward her and she froze, staring helplessly.

Run. Scream. Fight back. Do something. But she couldn't move. Stretched across the counter, Tyler made contact with her throat.

The front door opened, and Tyler was yanked away.

He was on his stomach on the floor before Brooke could even process what happened. Michael stood over him with his boot planted in the center of Tyler's back.

"Good afternoon, Hannah," Michael drawled. "Brooke will be taking the rest of the day off."

Chapter Six

Brooke huddled quietly in the passenger seat of Michael's SUV as they drove to her house. Though he'd swooped in and announced what she would be doing without consulting her, she didn't object. Take off work the rest of the day? Yes, sir. Get in the car? You bet.

The confrontation with Tyler had left her shaken. When he'd threatened her, she couldn't move, couldn't breathe. The very substantial wall she kept between herself and the rest of the world had shattered like thin glass, leaving her utterly vulnerable.

Clearly, Michael was more capable than she was of making decisions right now. And as much as she hated to think of herself as hopeless and fearful, she was grateful for Michael's decisive action. She couldn't remember another occasion when someone stepped forward to protect her like that. Her ex-husband had never even taken her side in an argument—he'd always been quick to point out why everything was her fault.

She glanced at Michael's profile as he drove with cool proficiency on the winding mountain roads. A muscle in his firm jaw twitched. Though he'd accepted her apology for leaving the courthouse instead of waiting for him, he still seemed angry. But she had the feeling that his hostility wasn't entirely aimed at her.

She asked, "How did your meeting with the FBI go?"

"Not good."

"Ditto," she said.

"Those two morons wouldn't even consider the possibility that there's a connection between Sally's murder and the others who have been killed."

The real reason for his anger was now apparent. The feds. Not her. She felt relieved.

"However," he said, "after what happened in the boutique, I'm beginning to think they might have a point. There's a lot of unanswered questions surrounding Sally's murder. I need to do my own investigation."

She wasn't sure that she liked that plan. "You don't trust the Pitkin County Sheriff's Office to handle it properly?"

"Deputy McGraw seems like a competent officer," he conceded. "And he's calling in the Colorado Bureau of Investigation to help with the lab work."

"Not to mention consulting with the FBI."

"Everybody is doing their job," he said impatiently. "And the fact of the matter is that I'm not here in an official capacity. I have no jurisdiction in this matter."

"But you still want to investigate. On your own."

"You bet. If I see something that needs investigating. I've always been a hands-on kind of person."

"A control freak?"

With a grin, he drawled, "I seem to recollect that I've been called a control freak before. Once or twice."

"It doesn't bother you?"

"Not when I'm the best person to handle the job." He glanced toward her. "We aren't all that different, you and me. You like to be in control. You want everything neat and tidy and done your way. Isn't that right?"

"Maybe." She did like things done a certain way but she lacked his confidence. Sensing that the conversation was veering into a deeper discussion about her past, she slipped into avoidance mode. "I'm glad we're going to my house because I really need to get fresh clothes. Is there anything else you hope to accomplish?"

"Never hurts to poke around," he said. "And I figure you might want to leave some notes for the cleaning crew."

"Notes?" He really must think she was a neatness fanatic. "I don't have special cleaning procedures."

"You might want them to box up Sally's belongings so they're ready to go when her parents arrive from New Zealand."

That meant sorting through her roommate's clothing and personal things. A difficult task but a necessary one, especially since Sally had been prone to claiming Brooke's possessions as her own. "Her parents are from New Zealand?"

"They spend winters there. Apparently, her family is fairly well off."

Though she hadn't thought of Sally as a rich kid, her roommate certainly wasn't in the poorhouse. Poor kids don't run away to Aspen to teach snowboarding. Sally had paid her share of the rent without blinking an eye and never seemed short of cash.

Michael pulled into her driveway. Sally's car was still there, but the area was otherwise deserted. The house looked forlorn with trampled, dirty snow and a strip of yellow crime scene tape draped across the door. "Is it okay for us to go inside?"

"I told McGraw that we'd be coming up here to get

some of your things, and he said it was fine. But he wanted the cleaning crew and the guy changing the locks to hold off until tomorrow afternoon. In case the CBI wanted to take a look around."

Going inside wouldn't be easy. She reminded herself that this was her home, her safe haven. It wasn't just a crime scene.

Michael placed his hand on her shoulder, and she turned toward him. His green eyes seemed to soften. As they gazed at each other, she yearned to be closer, to find solace in his arms. A sensation of warmth blossomed inside her and spread throughout her body. It had been years since she'd allowed herself to open up, since she'd trusted a man enough to let him get this close.

"You don't have to go inside," he said. "I can pick up what you need while you stay in the car."

But he couldn't sort through Sally's things. He had no way of knowing what belonged to her. "I should deal with Sally's stuff."

She was glad for his support as she unlocked the back door and entered the kitchen. The herd of policemen who tromped through her home last night had added to the mess. The floors were filthy. Drawers and cabinet doors were left open. The same uneasy sense of disarray permeated the living room. And the heavy rope still hung from the balcony.

Before she could become fixated on the noose, Michael nudged her toward the staircase. "Let's get this over with."

"I'm so glad my landlord isn't local. If he saw the place like this, I'd be evicted for sure."

In her own relatively tidy room, she found other evidence of police tampering. Her computer wasn't in its usual place. Several books that had been on shelves were on her bed. She was fairly sure they'd been through her drawers and her closet. "Why did they search in here?"

"Looking for evidence," he said. "It's what cops do. Nothing personal."

"Easy for you to say. Nobody went pawing through your underwear drawer."

She took a medium-sized suitcase from the closet and packed enough clothing for two or three days. In the bathroom, she grabbed her travel bag with the essentials. She opened the medicine cabinet and saw all of Sally's pain medications—cures for the bumps and bruises she suffered from snowboarding crash landings.

Michael stepped through the door with an empty shoe box. "Use this for Sally's things."

Was it necessary to pack Sally's electric toothbrush? Her hair dryer? Her deodorant? "Her family isn't going to want a half-used bottle of shampoo, right?"

"Don't try to make decisions," he advised. "Just pack up everything that belonged to your roommate. Everything you don't want to see again."

Quickly, she loaded the shoe box and took it into Sally's room where she found the usual chaos: magazines, used dishes and clothing scattered everywhere. She picked up a black camisole and held it by the straps, remembering how pretty the lacy edge had looked against Sally's pale skin. "She loved to get all dressed up."

"She was a pretty girl," Michael said.

"You never knew her."

"But she looked like you. That means she was pretty."

Though aware of his compliment, she was too caught up to acknowledge it. "Sorting through all this stuff. It's daunting."

"Just leave it," he said. "We'll tape a note on the door instructing the cleaning crew to box up everything in the room that isn't furniture."

Her gaze lit on her teal silk blouse. It seemed petty to dig through Sally's clothes, looking for those things that belonged to her. Would she ever want to wear them again?

"You write the note," she said. "I'm going to try to find clothes that Sally borrowed."

"Are you sure you want to—"

"Yes," she said decisively. "No time like the present."

Putting her emotions on hold, she sifted quickly through the piles of clothing. She found a couple of other shirts, a bottle of perfume, a necklace and a suede jacket. That was enough. If anything else accidentally got packed away with Sally's belongings, so be it.

As she picked up the jacket, she felt something in the pocket. Reaching inside, she found an unsealed, un-stamped envelope. The address written on the outside was for Damien Klinger in Denver. She showed it to Michael. "Sally's husband?"

"Could be. Open it."

She peeked and saw a personal check from Sally made out to Damien Klinger in the amount of one thousand dollars. "We should give this to the police."

"And we will. In time." He took the envelope and check from her and held them up. "This is where our investigation starts."

"Where?"

"Denver." He read the address aloud. "We're going to Denver."

"We?" How had she gotten swept up in his mission to ignore the authorities and solve the crime by himself? "I don't remember signing up for this investigation. Frankly,

I'm the worst person for the job. I don't like getting into other people's business, and I hate—no, make that despise—gossip. Everyone has a right to privacy. A right to be left alone."

"Even murderers?"

"That's not my point." When he was pushing his own agenda, he could be as irritating as a poison ivy rash. "Some people are born sleuths, and you're probably one of them. As for me? I'm an un-sleuth."

He chuckled, and she was irritated by how much she liked his laugh. "Un-sleuth?"

"I can't read people. My first impressions are almost always wrong." *Hence, my marriage and lousy choice of roommate.* "Somebody could confess to me, and I wouldn't even get it."

"I'm not asking you to be Sherlock Holmes. You don't have to say a word. Just stand there."

"If I'm not going to make myself useful, why should I go?"

"Because I'm not leaving you here in Aspen by yourself."

She scowled but was unable to argue, thinking of Tyler's hands closing around her throat.

"Until I know you're safe," he said, "I'm your bodyguard. If I go to Denver, you come with me."

"Control freak," she muttered. "This is a terrible idea. The police already talked to Sally's husband. He has an alibi."

"His girlfriend, who might have lied for him. Nobody else saw them." He waved the envelope like a flag. "I want to know why Sally was sending him this check."

She could think of a dozen perfectly innocent reasons why an estranged wife might be sending money to her husband. "Maybe she was repaying a loan. Maybe an investment. A mortgage payment on joint property."

"I'd like to hear what Damien Klinger has to say."

She groaned. Her preference for tonight would have been a long, hot soak in the hotel Jacuzzi and going to bed early. "Is it really worth a trip to Denver? It's a hundred and fifty miles. A four-hour drive."

He arched an eyebrow. "Who said anything about driving?"

ONCE AGAIN, Brooke had to revise her opinion of Michael Shaw. The man definitely had style and connections. With a few phone calls, he'd chartered a private jet from the Aspen Airport. And they were on their way.

Though she still wasn't thrilled about the idea of tracking down Sally's husband for their own investigation, she enjoyed being spontaneous. And she loved to fly.

As they soared into the clear skies, she peered through the porthole window beside her comfortable seat at the vast Rocky Mountains that surrounded them. The peaks and valleys, covered with snow, made a dramatic black-and-white scene. Rising to the edge of a few wispy clouds were distant peaks, majestic as glaciers.

"Mighty pretty country," Michael said.

"Shangri-la. A Utopian place of peace and solitude where dreams can come true."

"A good reason to come here. Searching for a dream. Or running from a nightmare."

"Or maybe," she said, changing the topic, "the mountains are just a fine place for sports. Do you ski?"

"Never appealed to me. Too cold."

She looked at him. Though the small cabin of the jet was ultra-plush and warm, he still wore his leather jacket.

"It's all about having the right clothes. There are all kinds of great fabrics that protect you from the weather without weighing you down."

"I suppose."

"I've been learning how to ski. Mostly sliding down the bunny slopes on my butt. Sally gave me a bunch of exercises to get into shape. Lots of stretches and lunges to build up my thigh muscles."

Inadvertently, she glanced toward his long, muscular legs, then quickly looked away. Michael was in excellent physical condition for any sport. Again, she had a vivid mental picture of Michael wearing only a pair of black boxers. Why was this image so clear? She'd never seen him like that.

An embarrassed flush crept up her neck and warmed her cheeks. She concentrated on the interior of the plane, willing the flush to recede. There were eight big chairs that adjusted for comfort and plenty of room to stretch out. Michael left his seat and went to the small kitchen area where he grabbed two bottled waters from the fridge. He held up prepackaged sandwiches. "We've got chicken salad, beef and vegan."

"Chicken salad, please."

He placed the food and drinks on the table in front of her and reconfigured his seat so they were facing each other. The setup reminded her of the motor homes her parents used to rent for family vacations. Only this was about a thousand times more luxurious.

She wondered if celebrities had been in this plane. Aspen was the winter playground of the rich and famous— jet-setters who routinely flitted across the country on a whim. Though Brooke hadn't yet met any of the "beautiful" people, Hannah cautioned her about gushing. Celebrities didn't come to Aspen to be recognized.

She picked up the chicken salad sandwich and noticed the "gourmet" sticker on the wrapping. "Even a sandwich is decadent on a private jet."

"I'd venture to guess that you know a little something about the lifestyles of the wealthy. Your ex-husband was a district attorney. So your job was probably to be involved in charity events and such."

"I've done my share of hobnobbing with the important people in Atlanta. My photo showed up in the society page a couple of times."

"Tell me about it."

"I'd rather not." Talking about those galas and balls would lead from one thing to another, and she didn't want to spill her guts to Michael—or anyone else for that matter.

"You promised to tell me about yourself," he reminded her. "You can't avoid this conversation forever."

"Sure I can." She smiled sweetly at him, but he didn't give an inch.

"Would you rather discuss our investigation?"

"No."

He watched her while he unwrapped his sandwich. His jade eyes were steady and cool. "Let's start with the reason you took out a restraining order on your ex-husband."

She decided to start at a different point in her autobiography. "Okay, here's my life story. I had a wonderful, normal childhood in Cleveland. Both of my parents were teachers. We spent many summers traveling around the country. I had an older brother and a golden retriever named Skippy."

"Why didn't you return to your parents' home after your difficult divorce?"

Because her marriage had failed. Because people like Brooke weren't supposed to get divorced, especially not after her huge society wedding with three hundred guests. "I wanted a change of scenery. A fresh start."

"In a place where nobody knew your name."

She took a sip of her bottled water. "When we had one of our family vacations in Colorado, I fell in love with the Rockies and always wanted to return."

. "That's a tidy rationale, Brooke. I have a sense that moving here was partly to hide from your most recent past."

"I'm not a coward." His incisive questions reminded her that he was a cop and was adept at interrogation. "Coming here was a declaration of independence. I'm taking charge of my own life."

"How long were you in therapy, Brooke?"

So casually, he lobbed this grenade. Her calm facade exploded. She couldn't pretend that her life had been the perfect embodiment of the American dream—not with this guy. "Good grief, Michael. Don't you know how to do small talk? Where's that famous Southern charm?"

He grinned. "You think I'm charming."

"When we first talked at the boutique, you were funny and interesting." Also sexy, which wasn't something she was ready to admit to him. "Can't we just have a pleasant little chat?"

"A chat? You're the one with the Southern charm. You sound like an old-fashioned lady sitting on the veranda doing needlepoint while Atlanta burns. My Aunt Hester was exactly like that. I remember her lying on her deathbed with her hair and makeup done."

"Aunt Hester again." Brooke was glad for an anecdote that had nothing to do with her. "Tell me about her."

"She refused to talk about her illness. Her last words were, 'I think I'll redecorate the kitchen in periwinkle blue.'"

"A lovely color." She sipped her water.

"Pretending that nothing was wrong didn't help." His drawl took on a harder edge. "When I first saw you, I didn't mention the real reason I'd come to Aspen. I didn't say one damned word about Robby Lee Warren. I wanted to be kind, to be a gentleman. And Sally died."

She heard an echo of her own self-reproach in his voice. Michael must be blaming himself for the murder—just like her. "You feel responsible."

"Damn right. Therefore, I sincerely hope you will forgive me if I don't want to discuss the weather or the headlines or the price of milk in Aspen. We need to talk about what's important."

Unfortunately, his logic made sense. She sighed. "Like what?"

"I'll ask the questions. You give the answers. Deal?"

She preferred to keep all her miserable memories locked inside, but it might be time to open the door and shine a light in the dark corners. Especially for Michael, who was working overtime to keep her safe. "I'll cooperate."

"Tell me about your therapy."

"While I was getting divorced, I started seeing someone, and she put me on a variety of antidepressants. Instead of making me feel better, I started having terrible nightmares. Even when I was awake."

"Delusions," he said. "Like at the house when you thought you saw an intruder?"

"I'm not crazy, Michael. Even though my ex-husband did his best to make it seem that way."

"Talk about him."

"Should I start with his infidelity? Or his constant reminders that I wasn't measuring up?" *Or that night in the hospital after the miscarriage when he blamed me?* She could have gone on and on, but she stopped. "Here's what happened when I left him. Thomas was embarrassed, and he didn't like it one bit. So he told outrageous lies about me. Then, he stalked me."

"That's when you took out the restraining order?"

"A fat lot of good it did." Though she'd left that life behind, bitterness remained, a nasty aftertaste on the back of her tongue. "Thomas was clever enough not to leave evidence. He'd follow me in his car. He'd break into my new apartment and move things. One time, he poured an entire bottle of his aftershave in my bathroom."

"When you told the police, they didn't believe you."

"I'd change the locks, and he'd find another way into the house. No one ever saw him. He was a like a ghost. A shadow." Until the night when he'd come into her bedroom, and everything she'd feared came true. She chased those thoughts out of her mind. "Nobody—not even my therapist—believed me."

"I do."

Was he leading her on? Pretending to believe her so she'd cooperate? Though she was lousy at reading people, she didn't think Michael was lying. But she'd already said too much. "What does the state of my mental health have to do with this murder, Michael?"

"Jackson Warren." Michael deliberately placed his sandwich on the table.

She shuddered as she remembered the photograph on Michael's computer. "What about him?"

"He's smart enough to bamboozle the FBI. They don't think of him as a serial killer because he's arranged each of these murders to be unique. He killed Grant with a bullet, execution-style. The second juror died in a supposed car accident. The third disappeared and hasn't been found. Sally's murder was supposed to look like a suicide."

"Which never made sense," she said. "Sally was a free spirit, romping through life without a care. Anybody who knew her would find it hard to believe that she killed herself. She just wasn't the type."

Michael reached across the table and took her hand. "What about you, Brooke? Are you the type of woman who might kill herself?"

"Of course not." Her response was immediate.

"Did your therapist ever ask you about suicidal thoughts?"

"Once or twice." *Maybe more often.*

"Which means you probably have a documented history of suicidal tendencies. Add to that the rumors spread by your ex-husband. And your troubles with the police."

She finally understood why Michael wanted to probe her past. Jackson Warren had constructed a scheme for murder based on her personal history. If Brooke had been found hanging from a noose, the investigation would turn up plenty of evidence to support suicide. Any number of people would have told Deputy McGraw that she was crazy. She could just hear Thomas telling everyone how tragic it was that she'd fallen apart.

"If he'd killed me instead of Sally, there wouldn't have been an investigation. He would have gotten away with murder."

"Again," Michael said.

Chapter Seven

The jet touched down at 5:25 p.m. at an airfield south of Denver. The rental car—gassed up and ready to roll—was waiting. Michael had handled the logistics of their trip perfectly. But he had made all kinds of mistakes with Brooke.

He'd driven her away by digging too deeply into her past. For a moment, she'd opened up to him. Just as quickly, she shut down. Her expressive face became as stiff as a mask, the light in her blue eyes went flat and she retreated inside herself. Yet she hadn't pulled her hand away when he touched her. And she'd given him information.

If he had months to learn about her, he would have been more careful. But he needed to know whether or not he could trust Brooke. Her erratic behavior led him to believe that she was damaged, possibly too damaged for him to handle. She'd admitted to delusions. She'd had two post-traumatic stress episodes while sleeping. More important, she refused to follow simple orders; she'd left the court-house after he told her to stay put. Those facts dictated that he ought to keep her on a short leash. Preferably locked up and sedated until he nabbed Jackson Warren and ended the threat.

But he'd also seen glimmers of strength and determination. His instincts told him that she was honest. He believed her when she said she'd been stalked by her ex-husband, and he gave her points for being sensible enough to seek therapy, for recognizing her problems, for taking control of her life by moving away from Atlanta.

Bottom line: He didn't think she was crazy. But she'd been hurt and was emotionally fragile. He needed to be more than a bodyguard, needed to carefully monitor her moods.

After he loaded her suitcase and laptop in the trunk of the rental car and slid behind the wheel, she spoke up. "Why are we here? I still see no point in talking to Sally's husband."

"He's a suspect." Michael turned the key in the ignition. "Murder investigations generally start with the spouse."

"I know," she said coldly. "My ex-husband liked to talk about his cases. And to point out that bad wives always get their just desserts."

He hated that she was citing her ex as an expert. The guy was the worst breed of bastard. Hiding his verbal abuse behind a sterling reputation, he'd strangled her with a velvet glove.

"Here's why we came to Denver. I want to know if Damien Klinger benefits—financially or otherwise—from his wife's death. I need to see his motives for myself. Is he a jealous man? What happened in their breakup? Was he the one who got dumped or was it the other way around?"

"But it's obvious how Sally died. Jackson Warren was the killer. He was coming after me, setting up a murder that looked like a suicide."

Michael consulted the navigational system in the car that showed the best route from the airfield to the address on the envelope. "That's one theory—not necessarily the *right* theory, though. There's always a chance that I could be mistaken."

"You? You might be wrong?"

The fact that she was teasing him was a good sign—maybe divulging all that personal information hadn't been so traumatic after all. "Even control freaks make the occasional error."

"Now that you mention it, I do see a flaw in your theory."

"Enlighten me."

"Sally and I resembled each other. But we weren't twins. If Jackson Warren is as smart as you think, how could he attack the wrong woman?"

"That's exactly what the feds are thinking," he said. "And Deputy McGraw. They think Sally was the intended victim."

For a moment, she was quiet. "On the other hand, your theory explains the murder method. Hanging is a complicated way to kill somebody. Why set up an elaborate hanging unless the purpose was to make it look like suicide?"

"Sally's husband might have thought the same thing."

"But she wasn't that type."

"We don't know that for sure," he said. "From what you've told me, Sally wasn't somebody who shared her secrets. She kept herself so busy with her parties and affairs that nobody could really get close."

"Ironic," she said. "Sally and I appeared to be very different personalities, but we were both guarded."

"Like Fort Knox."

Her light laugh surprised him. "What's so funny?"

"Your comparison. Thinking of women as fortresses."

She smirked. "I'm guessing it's been a while since you've been in a relationship."

"Could be."

He merged into rush hour traffic on the highway that seemed to be moving at a fairly steady pace. She was right about his lack of female companionship. He dated, but there was nothing long term. "My sister says I'm hopeless, that I'm too much of a workaholic to ever settle down."

"Is she? Settled down?"

"Oh, yeah. Five years ago, she married another scientist. They're highly compatible. Even have matching lab coats."

"Any children?"

"That's next on my sister's agenda. With her, everything has to be planned."

"Another control freak?" She rolled her eyes. "You two must have fought all the time when you were growing up."

"Like badgers with a bone."

When he glanced over at Brooke, he noticed how the late afternoon sunlight caught the rich, red highlights in her silky hair. Her mood had lightened, as if the warmer weather at lower elevation had melted the cold regret of her memories. When she met his gaze and smiled, his pulse jumped. She was an amazingly attractive woman.

"How can I help?" she asked.

His mind was so occupied with the surge of desire he felt, and his overwhelming need to touch her that he could barely understand her question. "Help?"

"With Sally's husband. Remember, I told you that I'd make a lousy detective. You're going to have to give me some guidance."

He reined in his thoughts and concentrated on the traffic. "Actually, you could be very helpful. Since I don't have jurisdiction in Colorado, I can't compel Damien to talk to me. He might be more sympathetic to you as Sally's roommate."

"Especially if I hand him a check for a thousand bucks."

"Let's hold off on mentioning the money. The check is evidence that needs to be turned in to McGraw."

"How should I start? Are there any special interrogation techniques? Can we do the good-cop, bad-cop thing?"

"You're joking, right?"

She laughed. "It might be fun to play detective. And it's a relief to be in Denver, a hundred and fifty miles away from anybody who might want me dead."

"Not to mention that it's forty degrees warmer here."

He hadn't minded driving in the Aspen snow, but it was pleasant to cruise along a highway with nothing more to worry about than the other cars. After he exited, his GPS directions showed only a few more miles to the address on the envelope.

He drove into a quiet residential neighborhood that felt as comfortable as an old shoe. The houses were mostly brick on a street with tall, old trees that had lost their leaves. Damien Klinger's house was a bungalow, set back from the curb. Pleasant enough but nothing spectacular.

"Do you think he's home?" Brooke asked.

"He's there." He pointed to a vanity plate that said "Damien" on a Toyota parked at the curb.

"Clever detective work."

They walked side by side up the walk. Michael rang the doorbell and stepped back. The idea of using Brooke to gain access was beginning to fell like a good one.

The door opened quickly, as if the short blond man who answered had been expecting someone else. Though he'd taken off his necktie, he was still dressed for the office in beige trousers and a white shirt, rolled up at the sleeve. Standing behind the screen door, he peered through wire-rimmed glasses, looking closely at Brooke. "Can I help you?"

"Are you Damien Klinger?" Michael asked.

He nodded.

Brooke introduced herself as Sally's roommate, adding, "I'm so sorry for your loss."

He frowned. "Thanks."

"May we come in?"

He pushed open the screen. "Just for a minute. I'm expecting someone."

The interior of the small house was simple and un-adorned, except for two orange pillows with Denver Broncos logos. Every piece of furniture faced the flat-screen TV.

"Have you been in touch with Sally's parents?" Brooke asked.

"They're arriving tomorrow from New Zealand," he said. "They'll be taking care of the, um, arrangements. Sally and I were separated."

"This must be uncomfortable for you," Brooke said with exactly the right level of sympathy.

As Michael watched, Brooke used her skill at small talk to pull responses from Sally's estranged husband. Damien seemed to be a regular guy with an average life, an average job at an engineering firm and season tickets to the Broncos. The creases on his forehead and at the corners of his eyes made Michael think he was older than Sally. Maybe in his early forties. Bland and normal, Damien paled in comparison to Sally's latest flame, Tyler Hennessey.

Brooke hit a nerve when she mentioned how Sally always left a mess.

"She was a pig," Damien said angrily. "During the five years we were married, she never put away a single dish. I couldn't stand it. We separated twice before this last time when she moved to Aspen. Good riddance, I say."

He looked down for a moment, aware that he might have said too much. "Look, I'm sorry she's dead, but—"

"In Aspen, she taught snowboarding at the ski school," Brooke said. "What did she do here in Denver?"

"Sales."

"What kind?"

"You name it. Sometimes legitimate. Sometimes not. Sally always liked working the angles, putting something over on someone." He shook his head. "That doesn't sound good, does it? I don't mean to say bad things about her, but Sally had a real nasty streak."

Now that he'd opened up, Michael moved in with his own questions. "Were you aware that she was dating?"

"Aware? She flaunted her boyfriends." His chin lifted. "I don't care. I've found someone special of my own."

"Were you going to file for divorce?"

"I still had a few issues with Sally."

"Financial issues," Michael guessed.

Damien eyed Michael for a moment. "Why are you asking me these questions? What do you want?"

"We just happened to be in town," Brooke said smoothly. "I thought we'd stop by and tell you that I found a check Sally had written to you. In the amount of one thousand dollars."

"Where is it?"

"Right now, it's evidence," Michael said.

"Swell," he muttered. "I'll probably never see the cash.

Sally owed me six thousand, six hundred and thirty-seven dollars for her car. That was the last scam she pulled on me."

"That's why you couldn't divorce her," Michael said. "You were hoping to get some of your money back."

"I knew it wouldn't do much good to go through a lawyer. She always claimed to be broke."

"Where do you think she got the money?"

He gave a bitter laugh. "She was probably playing some other poor sucker. His loss."

The doorbell rang. Before Damien could answer, a woman with short brown hair stepped inside. When she moved to Damien's side and took his arm, Michael noticed that they fit together nicely. He introduced her as his girlfriend, a fourth grade teacher.

Michael's first impression was that this woman had never told a lie in her life, much less provided Damien with a false alibi.

With a friendly smile, she shook both their hands. Her gaze lingered on Brooke. "You must be related to Sally. You look just like her photographs."

BROOKE STARED into the mirror above the bathroom sink in their Denver hotel suite. Did she really look that much like Sally? The only similarity she saw was the color of their hair and eyes. She ran her finger down the length of her nose. Sally's was more blunt, and her smile stretched all the way across her face. Brooke's lips were fuller.

Yet Damien's girlfriend was the latest in a long line of people who had commented on the similarity. Jackson could have made the same mistake.

She hated to consider that possibility but there was an air of inevitability about Michael's theory. One bad thing led to another, and her life path was, apparently, the road to ruin.

She turned on the hot water in the tub. Once again, Michael had made first-class accommodations. She had to give him kudos for taste. Though he could drive her crazy in many ways—like when he tried to run her life for her—she couldn't deny her attraction to him. And she was discovering new things to like about him all the time. When he wanted to be, he was incredibly charming. On their way into the restaurant for dinner, he'd placed his hand near the small of her back to guide her. His touch felt exactly right. He'd kept the dinner conversation light with lots of long, involved stories about all the characters in his family. His late aunt Hester, the Southern belle. Uncle Elmo and his legendary hunting dog Jo-Jo. Michael's sister and her scientist husband. And his widowed mother. The talk of family made her miss her own relatives back in Cleveland.

Michael clearly adored his family. He had the gallantry of a Southern gentleman, and she was even beginning to like his accent despite the memories it brought back of her life in the South.

Though her attraction to him was growing, she would spend tonight the same way she had spent last night—separated from him by a closed door. The last thing she needed right now was to get caught up in her feelings for Michael. She planned to have a nice, long soak and then to go to bed. It was only nine, but she was plenty tired—it would be easy to fall asleep. The hard part came later, when she dreamed. Last night was a nonstop horror show, and she wasn't looking forward to a rerun.

With her hair swept up on top of her head, she eased into the steaming water, hoping to lie back and enjoy the luxury surrounding her.

She sank in the water up to her chin. *Relax, Brooke. You have nothing to fear.* Like a mantra, she repeated the words: *Nothing to fear, nothing to fear.* The danger was far away, back in Aspen. She closed her eyes.

The intruder's face swam behind her eyelids. She saw him appearing in the dark outside the window, as distorted and grotesque as a gargoyle. His features morphed into the photograph of Jackson. Was it him? Had he been that close? She shook her head and saw Tyler Hennessey reaching for her throat. Then she saw Thomas.

She sat up straight and rubbed her eyes. There was no reason to be afraid. Not now. Not here.

Every time she succumbed to fear, it felt like Thomas had won another battle in the war. Anger sent a jolt of energy through her veins. She was tired of the fact that he could still scare her. It was time to calm down and get some sleep.

She slipped into a soft nightshirt and pulled back the forest green covers on the bed. But when she went to turn out the light, she found she couldn't do it. She had no interest in being in the dark. She grabbed her cell phone off the nightstand instead and checked her messages.

There was a call from Hannah, telling her not to worry about coming to work, and three other messages from people she barely knew who wanted to offer condolences.

These contacts were evidence that she wasn't completely isolated. If she fell off the face of the earth, someone would notice. But it wasn't enough to calm her mind.

She flopped back against the pillows. *Go to sleep.* But as soon as she closed her eyes, she saw the face of a serial killer. The noose that hung from her balcony. Thomas.

Usually, Brooke preferred to handle her fears by herself. But that didn't seem to be an option tonight.

Tonight, she couldn't be alone.

Chapter Eight

Brooke opened the door and found Michael on the sectional sofa, his long legs stretched out in front of him. In his casual jeans and black V-neck sweater, he looked utterly at home in the elegant surroundings. The glow from a chrome table lamp highlighted his cheekbones and stubborn chin.

Her gaze fell to his hands—well-shaped with long, artistic fingers—and she remembered those capable hands clenched around a pistol. Now he held a glass, half-filled with amber liquid.

He raised his glass and smiled. She felt a blush heat her face, and she pulled the hotel bathrobe around her a little tighter. "I'm having bourbon. Can I get you something from the minibar?"

She considered it. A few shots of booze might help her fall asleep, but alcohol would also lower her inhibitions, which could cause any number of problems. "I'll stick to water."

Disregarding the unpleasant thought that a bottled water from a minibar probably cost ten bucks, she helped herself and then settled on the sofa, far enough away from Michael that there was no chance of accidentally touching him.

"Damien Klinger," she said, crossing her bare legs and arranging the robe to cover them. "Definitely not a murderer."

Michael sipped his bourbon. "I thought you preferred to keep the topic of murder off-limits."

Though she'd carefully held her fears at bay throughout dinner, there was no escape. As soon as she'd closed her eyes in the tub, the demons appeared in all their grotesque glory. It might be better to face them head-on.

"Changed my mind," she said with a breeziness she didn't really feel. "If I'm going to help you investigate, I should start thinking like a detective."

"Then allow me to compliment you on the way you handled Damien. You did a fine job of loosening him up. We learned a lot from him."

"We did?"

"He told us that Sally had a nasty streak and didn't mind using people."

Brooke already knew about those aspects of her roommate's personality. "What else?"

"Finances," he said. "She had enough money that she intended to make a payment on her debt to Damien. Maybe from a wealthy boyfriend."

"Tyler Hennessey." Brooke ignored the shudder that ran up her spine. "I don't know how much a professional snowboarder makes for competing, but he's a star. Probably does endorsements."

"A boatload of endorsements." Michael got up and grabbed his laptop, bringing it over to the coffee table in front of the sofa. He hit a key and a picture of a tanned, smiling Tyler with streaky blond hair appeared. "Snowboarding is big business with big bucks attached."

He clicked on a video of a snowboarder zooming into

a half pipe of glare ice. Careening from one side to the other, he flew high above the edge. In the air, he performed gravity-defying flips and twists.

"Is that Tyler?"

"Sure is." Michael leaned forward to watch. "He's good. Gets a lot of air, maybe twenty-five or thirty feet."

"I thought you weren't big on winter sports."

"This is pretty much like a skateboard on snow," Michael said.

She shot him a skeptical glance. With his neatly trimmed brown hair and glass of bourbon, he certainly didn't look like a typical skateboarding dude. "You skateboard?"

"I got into it when I was a rookie cop, thinking I could relate to the kids. I'm no Tony Hawk, but I'm not half bad." He grinned. "While I'm in Aspen, I might have to give this snowboarding a try."

That sounded like a long-range plan. "How long are you planning to stay?"

"As long as it takes," he said, giving Brooke a pointed stare that made her stomach flip. He returned to the photo. "Our boy Tyler has his handsome mug on several different products. His nickname is Lightning. Like the tattoo on his wrist."

"Or his obviously dyed blond hair," she said.

"His reputation is that he's a successful athlete with a bad attitude. He doesn't like to lose. If he thought Sally was playing him for a fool, he might have lashed out at her."

"An abusive personality. But men who have trouble controlling their rage don't usually plan their assaults."

"Crime of passion," he said.

She'd always found that to be an odd phrase; she associated passion with love. "More like a crime of rage."

"We'll keep Tyler on the radar as a suspect," he said. "But I keep coming back to Jackson."

And so did she. No matter how much she would have preferred to believe another theory—one that didn't involve an ongoing threat to her life—Stonewall Jackson Warren seemed the most likely suspect. "I still don't understand how this supposedly intelligent killer made the mistake of attacking Sally instead of me."

"I figured it out." He rose to his feet. "Stand up, and move over there by the desk."

Though wary, she did as he said. "What are you going to do?"

"A reenactment. Now face the wall."

She turned. "This isn't going to hurt, is it?"

He grinned at her. "I'll be gentle, I promise. Now suppose you're Sally and you've gone into your roommate's bedroom to see if she's got any clothes you want to borrow."

"That would be typical."

"Pretend like you're looking in the closet."

She could feel him coming closer. "Wait. Wouldn't Sally have heard him approach?"

"Not if she was playing music."

"Too true. She always had the volume on high."

"The killer sneaks into the house and climbs the staircase. He knows which one is your bedroom."

"How does he know that?"

"He's been watching."

"A stalker," she said, cringing at the thought.

"He steps inside your bedroom and sees a woman with auburn hair. He recognizes the wristwatch." She felt him coming closer. In a quiet voice, he said, "The Pitkin County coroner found a needle mark on Sally's throat. She was probably injected with a sedative."

His arm encircled her throat, and he pulled her back against his chest. The full body contact had an instant effect. She was aware of his strength, of the hard muscles in his torso and arms. A vibrating heat radiated from his body to hers.

She forced herself to speak. "Is this the part where you inject me?"

"Exactly right."

The timbre of his deep voice resonated inside her, filling the void of loneliness she'd lived with for years. A small moan crept up the back of her throat. "I see."

"But the killer didn't. He could have attacked Sally without ever seeing her face."

He released his hold, and she turned toward him. They were close, so close that she could see the patterns in his green eyes. Their bodies were almost touching. She wanted to kiss him. But that was out of the question. Sheer craziness. She wasn't a wild-eyed teenager who couldn't control her urges, and there were a dozen logical reasons why she shouldn't act on this impulse. Michael wasn't part of her life. He lived all the way across the country in Alabama. They couldn't have a relationship.

But a kiss? Just one kiss?

Without breaking eye contact, she slid both hands up his chest. The contrast between his soft cashmere sweater and the firm muscles of his chest excited her—he was a Christmas present waiting to be unwrapped. Her arms circled his neck.

He leaned down. His mouth slid across hers. On his lips, she tasted the bourbon. Sharp. Tingling. Intoxicating.

The hard pressure of his kiss stole her breath away. His arms captured her, holding her tightly as he kissed her again. Slowly, sensually, his tongue explored her mouth. Never before had she been kissed like this. Never.

Every cell in her body responded to his caresses. There was no holding back now, even if she wanted to. She needed to experience every delicious sensation. Fireworks exploded in whirling pinwheels behind her eyelids. She heard chimes.

Michael leaned away from her. "What's that noise?"

With a start, she recognized her ringtone. "My cell phone."

The ringing stopped, but the interruption had given her enough time to regain control. These kisses had knocked her off balance and set her on a path she realized she wasn't ready to be on, no matter what her body said.

When the ringtone sounded again, she broke free from his embrace and ran into the bedroom to answer. Breathless, she said, "Hello?"

"What the hell are you trying to pull?"

Thomas. It was Thomas. Her heart stopped.

"Don't play games with me, Brooke. You know better."

She heard the threat in his voice so clearly that he could have been standing outside the door to their hotel room. "Where are you?"

"Did you think I wouldn't find out?" He gave a harsh laugh. "I knew. The minute your boyfriend called the Atlanta PD to check up on me, I knew. I don't need those damn insinuations about my character."

"I don't know what you're talking about."

"Never call down here again. That goes double for your meddling boyfriend. You can both go straight to hell."

He disconnected the call.

In shock, she stared at her cell phone. In the brief span of a few moments, she'd plummeted from a starlit high in Michael's arms straight into the gutter. The voice of her ex-husband repulsed her, enraged her. He had no right to contact to her. Not now. Not ever again. She flung the cell phone onto the bed and charged into the living room where Michael was pouring himself another drink from the minibar.

Struggling with her anger, she asked, "Did you call Atlanta?"

"Who was on the phone?"

"Thomas."

He cursed under his breath. "You should have let me talk to him."

"Oh, I think you've done quite enough talking. Thomas said that someone—someone identifying himself as my boyfriend—made a call to the Atlanta Police Department."

He calmly lifted the drink to his mouth and took a taste. Standing in this elegant suite, he looked so perfect that she could just spit.

She demanded an answer. "Was it you? Did you make that call?"

"I spoke to a cop I know in Atlanta. He was one of the detectives investigating Grant's murder."

"Why?"

"I needed information." A muscle in his jaw twitched. "I made the call this morning, long before you told me what really happened when you took out a restraining order."

"You were checking up on me." She couldn't believe his nerve. "You wanted to get his opinion on whether or not I was crazy."

"If you recall," he said in an infuriatingly slow drawl, "you weren't exactly forthcoming with the details of your past. I needed to know what I was dealing with."

"So you pried into my past. Without my permission. And you opened a can of worms."

He didn't even try to defend his actions. How could he? There was no excuse for what he'd done. He had violated her privacy and she would never trust him again.

"Damn it, Michael. How could you?"

She turned on her heel, went into the bedroom and firmly closed the door.

STARING AT the closed door, he finished his drink in one swig. Two bourbons in one night. Not a good sign.

Brooke was driving him insane. First she resented him, then accepted him, then blamed him. And then—wonder of wonders—she kissed him. She'd initiated the physical contact, of that he was certain—as much as he'd wanted to embrace her, he had purposely held himself back. It wouldn't have been appropriate, especially given her history. He hadn't wanted to pressure her.

But she had kissed him. And her body came alive in his arms. She was trembling, gasping with excitement.

Then the phone rang and—once again—everything was his fault. The woman opened up and shut down faster than a swinging door.

He'd had enough. Without knocking, he stormed into her bedroom. "Listen up, Brooke. I know your life has been hard. You've been mistreated and misunderstood. But I'm not the bad guy."

Her eyes flashed. "Get out."

"I came here to protect you."

"Or to accuse me."

"Never," he growled. "I never laid blame on you."

"You thought I was nuts. You called Atlanta to verify that opinion."

"I won't apologize for making that call. I needed information. That's what I do. I'm a cop. I gather evidence. It was for your own—"

"Stop!" She planted her fists on her hips. "Don't you dare say that it was for my own good."

"I had to find out in order to know how to protect you!"

"If you'd decided—in your great and arrogant wisdom— that I was a fruitcake, what did you intend to do? Put me in a straitjacket?"

"I sure as hell wouldn't have taken you along on an interrogation. I wouldn't have discussed the murder with you. But you're not crazy."

"Thanks for the vote of confidence," she said. "I'm more than 'not crazy,' Michael. I'm a competent, strong woman."

Her statement would have been a whole lot more effective if she hadn't been wearing a baby-blue, knee-length nightshirt with dancing sheep all over it. Still, he said, "I'm not underestimating you."

"That's not what it sounds like."

The air between them crackled with electricity. Her cheeks flamed with color. As she glared at him, her features sharpened with a fierce intensity. He saw the strength she'd spoken of, recognizing the will of a survivor. "Anger becomes you."

"What?"

"You're a fighter. That's good. That's what you're going to need to get through this."

"A fighter." She exhaled the breath she'd been holding. "I'm glad you see me that way."

"Listen, Brooke, I regret that your ex-husband heard about my inquiry and misinterpreted the purpose. I'm sorry you had to put up with a call from that snake."

"Hearing his voice…" She stopped, shaking her head. "He sickens me."

Michael noticed that she'd let her guard down a bit. He offered, "If you want to talk about your divorce—"

"I don't."

"It helps to talk about the things that hurt. To let go."

She scoffed. "You sound like my shrink."

"No analysis," he said, raising a hand to fend off her allegation. "I deal with facts, and I'm speaking from experience."

"And?"

"I know about trauma. People need to tell the stories of their own personal hell. Maybe once. Maybe twice. Maybe a hundred times. As much as it takes. If you talk about your demons, they lose that power." He looked her straight in the eye. "Talk to me, Brooke."

"Not now." She folded her arms across her chest. "All I want is to be back home in Aspen. In my own house. In my own bed."

"Tomorrow night," he promised. "By then, the cleaning crew and the locksmith should be done."

"Okay."

"And I will be staying with you. Until Sally's murder is solved, I'm your bodyguard."

No matter what she said or how much she protested. He would stay at her side.

Chapter Nine

The next morning, Brooke stumbled onto the private jet and collapsed in her seat. All night she'd heard echoes of her ex-husband's voice in her head. She'd even constructed an elaborate scenario about Thomas coming to Aspen to kill her. Impossible, of course. He was a high-profile, important mucky-muck who couldn't leave the state of Georgia without someone taking notice. His nearness was only in her mind.

As soon as they were airborne, Michael went to the kitchenette area and picked up a carafe. "More coffee?"

She'd already had two cups. "Do you have sugar?"

"You like three packets," he said. "Mighty sweet."

She shrugged. "If the caffeine doesn't get me going, the sugar will."

"You had a rough night. I heard you tossing around."

Which meant that he had also been awake. But he looked perfectly refreshed—clean-shaven and neatly dressed in a brand-new shirt he'd purchased at the hotel shop. He was probably one of those guys who function like a charm with only a couple hours of sleep. She certainly didn't fall into that category. Her lack of rest showed in the dark circles under her eyes.

When he poured coffee into a white mug and placed it on the table in front of her, she caught a whiff of his after-shave. The scent brought back their kiss and the way his lips had felt on hers. She shook off the memory before it got the better of her.

"We're going to make another stop before we go to Aspen," he said. "I need to see someone in Salt Lake City."

Before she could complain about the way he consistently made plans without consulting her, he added, "Do you mind?"

"I guess not," she said, trying not to be petulant. It made sense to use the jet while he had it chartered. Why not Salt Lake City? Why not Singapore? "Who are you planning to see?"

"Her name is Tammy Gallegos. She was on your jury panel."

Brooke recalled a well-dressed woman in her twenties. "Blond hair and brown eyes? Very attractive?"

"That's her." He poured a coffee for himself and sat opposite her. "You and Tammy are the only two jurors who departed from the Atlanta area. I figured that while I was in this part of the country, I might as well visit her and see if there's any way I can improve her security."

"Do you think Jackson will go after her?"

"Maybe not right away. He seems to be following the order of the jury list, and Tammy was farther down the line. But Salt Lake City isn't too far from Aspen. He could drive there in six or seven hours on the highway."

She sucked down a gulp of her ultra-sweetened coffee, hoping for a burst of alertness. "Have you warned the other jurors in Atlanta?"

He nodded. "I've been in contact. In spite of the FBI's lack of interest, most everybody took me seriously."

"A threat to your life will do that," she said. "Why don't you just call Tammy? Why is it necessary to see her in person?"

"The crackpot factor." He grinned at her. "How would you have felt if you got a phone call out of the blue telling you that you were in danger?"

"A little creeped out."

"Then you would have forgotten all about it," he said. "An in-person visit makes a stronger impression. And I don't present myself as alarmist. I venture to say that I look like a fairly trustworthy individual."

"I thought so until I got to know you." She finished off the dregs of her coffee. "Then, much to my surprise, I find out that you're really a gnarly skateboarder dude."

In spite of the coffee and the unexpected side trip to Salt Lake City, Brooke began to relax. The slight motion of the jet soothed her and she could feel her eyes closing.

"Your seat reclines," he said. "If you want to catch a couple of Zs, go ahead."

"Maybe I'll just rest my eyes."

The thrum of the engines reminded her of the soothing sound of a gentle surf. She imagined a sunlit beach and warm water lapping at white sands. Palm trees swayed in the breeze. The sky overhead was a soft aquamarine.

Purposefully, she relaxed her toes, her ankles, her knees. And she listened to the surf. Her fingers unclenched. Her head rolled back against the seat.

The waves rippled. The sun shone down. She and Thomas had honeymooned for an idyllic week in the Greek Islands. *Thomas. Thomas.* His name caused storm clouds to appear on the horizon. Rolling waves of thunder crashed through her mind. She was in danger, running hard, struggling to escape. But her feet stuck in the sand. Every step took an effort.

A heavy fishing net dropped from the sky, weighing her down. Her arms and legs tangled in the wet ropes. She fought with all her might but couldn't move.

This is only a dream. I can wake up…

She was in the bedroom she'd shared with Thomas. The lamp on the bedside table cast distorted shadows against the cream-colored wall. She'd cut her hand. Blood oozed onto the carpet.

He came closer. The pain came closer.

"No." She forced herself to stand. "Get away from me."

Only a dream…

She forced her eyes open. Saw the interior of the jet. Felt the vibration of the floor beneath her feet.

"Brooke."

Michael. He stood across the table from her, reaching toward her with deep empathy in his eyes. She hated that he'd seen her like this. "I'm okay," she said. "In spite of what you're thinking, I'm okay."

"Do you know where we are?"

"Of course." She rested her hand on the back of her chair. When had she stood up? Had she been acting out her dream? "I hope I didn't do anything ridiculous. Sleep-walking or something."

"Tell me what happened."

"It was only a nightmare." She tried to brush it off. "One of those silly nightmares about—"

"Tell me about Thomas," he interrupted. "You said his name."

She had only related these events to one other person— her therapist. The truth was too humiliating to share with anyone else.

"What else did I say? Maybe I clucked like a chicken?" She attempted to make a joke, although she couldn't laugh right now if somebody paid her.

Michael lowered himself into his seat. "We don't need to talk about your nightmare. I want to know about you. Your real life. Something terrible happened between you and Thomas. He hurt you."

She straightened her spine. "The abuse—my ex-husband's abuse—was more than verbal. More than the stalking."

"Go on," he said.

Unable to look at him, her gaze focused on the carpeted floor of the jet. "On the night I left him, we had just come home from a political fund-raising event. Thomas had been drinking, but I'd had only one glass of wine, early in the evening. I insisted on driving home."

She remembered the argument in the car. He'd found fault with her driving, even though there was nothing to complain about. "When we got to the house, I went inside and straight upstairs to the bedroom. He came up behind me, cursing. He spun me around and slapped me hard."

Her eyes were dry—she'd already shed an ocean of tears—but her cheeks burned. "He shoved me. Tore my dress. When I screamed, he slapped me again. I fell to the floor. I held up my hand to protect myself, and his diamond pinkie ring cut my hand. I was bleeding on the carpet, and that made him even more angry. He kicked me."

Her voice trailed off. For a moment, she stood in silence. "Here's the worst part. On some level, I knew. I knew that our arguments would ultimately end in violence. I should have left him before it got to that point."

"Brooke, you couldn't have known—"

"I could have. I should have." Now that she'd finally

started talking, she couldn't seem to stop. "I refused to believe that the man I loved—my husband—could do such a thing. In spite of all the warning signs, I chose to be blind. And stupid."

"You're not stupid."

"How else can I explain it? A person like me has no excuse for allowing herself to be a battered wife."

"It wasn't your fault." His voice was low, gentle. "You didn't do anything wrong. And it will never happen again."

"It's happening now, Michael. I'm being stalked and terrorized. Again."

"This time, you're not helpless." He left his chair and took her hand. "Your eyes are wide open."

When she met his gaze, she saw something in the set of his jaw, something in his attitude that reassured her more than words. "You're right, Michael. This is different. I'm stronger now. And I'm not alone. I've got you."

This threat had nothing to do with her actions or lack of decision. She couldn't blame herself.

This time truly was different.

Only the fear felt the same.

IN SALT Lake City, Michael was pleased to find Tammy Gallegos working in a secure building. At the entrance, he and Brooke passed by uniformed security guards with X-ray machines and metal detectors. While at work, Tammy couldn't have been safer.

Her office was located on the seventh floor. Though she came out from behind her desk to shake hands with both of them, he noticed a wariness in her dark brown eyes. With her short, straight blond hair and her crisp gray pantsuit, she appeared every inch a businesswoman—

someone who was likely to disregard warnings that didn't fit into her neat, tidy world.

Once again, he opted to step back and allow Brooke to handle the initial conversation. Her natural charm would put Tammy at ease.

"I remember the trial," Tammy said. "And I definitely remember you, Brooke. You were so cool and classy, and I was an out-of-work computer analyst, fresh out of grad school and newly married. I almost asked you for a job recommendation."

"Looks like you've done well for yourself," Brooke said.

"You're different, too."

Michael watched as Tammy eyed Brooke's casual sweater and jeans, taking her measure. He was interested in what she might have to say about the changes in Brooke's life.

"I moved to Aspen," Brooke said. "I live in an A-frame on the side of a cliff."

"Mountain living suits you. You look…free. Like you blew in here on a fresh breeze."

"Not many people would say that I'm a free and breezy person," Brooke said, laughing.

Michael could tell that she was gratified to be described in such a manner, even if she didn't really think it were true.

"What does your company do?" Brooke asked.

"Worldwide oil exploration and distribution. I handle office systems. My husband works here, too. He's a geologist," she beamed. "There's a lot of travel involved. Tomorrow night, we're both leaving for Kuwait."

"Wow, that's an exotic assignment."

"And I'm kind of in a rush, actually." Tammy glanced

at her desk, which was piled high with folders. "I have tons of paperwork to clean up before I go. What was it you needed to tell me?"

Michael stepped forward. "Why don't we all sit down for just a minute."

Wary again, she took a seat behind her desk while he explained about the death of Robby Lee Warren and the subsequent murders of three jurors. While he spoke, Tammy kept glancing at Brooke for confirmation.

Her manicured fingernails tapped nervously on a manila folder. "And you think this Stonewall Jackson person might come after me?"

"It's possible," Brooke said.

"He killed your roommate?"

"We think so," Brooke repeated. "But her murder is still under investigation. It could turn out to be unrelated, though the fact that Sally and I looked so much alike leads us to believe otherwise."

"Better to be safe than sorry," Tammy said.

Michael appreciated her decisiveness. She'd accepted his story far more quickly than most. "Have you noticed anyone watching you? Anything out of the ordinary?"

Her forehead tensed in a frown. "There was an incident last night at our condo. Someone disabled the security cameras in the underground parking garage. Did you say that the second juror was killed in a faked car accident?"

"That's right," Michael said.

"I'll tell my husband," she promised. "And I'll take pre-cautions."

"It's fortunate that you're leaving town," Brooke said. "You'll probably be safer in the Middle East than in this country."

"That's always true. My company goes to extraordinary

measures to protect employees on assignment. We always have bodyguards and a secure residence."

She rose and Tammy and Brooke gave each other a friendly hug, promising to stay in touch. It hardly seemed possible that this self-possessed Brooke was the same woman who suffered from debilitating nightmares and delusions. He was proud of the way Brooke was handling herself during their investigation.

On the way out of the building, she said, "I'm glad we had a chance to warn her."

"It's great that she's leaving the country."

"Do you think Jackson messed with the security cameras at her condo?"

"Maybe," he said.

"The timing works. He could have left Aspen and driven here yesterday." She shrugged. "Then again, it could be something entirely unrelated. Nothing to worry about."

"Never say that."

"You want me to worry?" she asked.

"I want you to be vigilant."

As they stepped out into the midday sun, he scanned the plaza. Jackson Warren could be here in Salt Lake City, hiding in the shadows, picking his moment to attack.

Michael's hand went automatically to the place on his belt where his holster should have been. He'd left his gun in the rental car when he saw the security setup at Tammy's building. A mistake? Jackson Warren could be watching them through a rifle's telescopic lens.

But that wasn't his style. A sniper shooting in the middle of Salt Lake City would be heavily investigated. The feds would get involved.

Still, the hair on the back of Michael's neck prickled as he took Brooke's arm and hurried her to the car.

Chapter Ten

The threat Michael had sensed in Salt Lake City multiplied a hundred times when they returned to Aspen, the scene of the crime. Coming back here felt like stepping out of the wind and into the eye of a tornado.

On the jet, he'd suggested to Brooke that she come back to Birmingham with him for Christmas. They could spend the holiday at his family's estate, which included the farming operation and his sister's labs. All those lands were well-protected.

She'd refused, of course, because nothing in life was easy.

Immediately, he started pushing a second option, which was to stay at the hotel—a more easily controlled environment. As he held open the door to their suite, he touted the comfort and convenience of his plan. "The hotel is closer to where you work."

"Don't care."

"You could order every meal from room service."

"And gain twenty pounds?" She shook her head. "I don't think so."

"Staying here would be like a vacation. Jacuzzis every day. Maid service. Mints on the pillow."

He followed her into the living room where she stretched out on the long sectional sofa. When she looked up at him, determination radiated from her pretty blue eyes. "I want to go home. To my own house."

"I hate negotiating."

"Most control freaks do," she said sweetly.

He abandoned the pretense that staying here would be like a visit to a spa. "You know the real reason I want you in the hotel. It's safer. There's only one entrance to this suite. The windows don't open onto balconies. We're closer to the police."

"Very practical," she agreed.

"And you are a practical woman."

"Used to be," she mused. "Maybe I'm turning all free and breezy, like Tammy said."

"Fine. You can go wafting around on fairy wings. Let me worry about the danger." As he stood looking down at her, a wave of protectiveness surged through him. Keeping her safe was becoming more than a duty. He cared about her, more deeply than he wanted to admit. "As your bodyguard, I advise you to move into the hotel with me."

"For how long?"

"Until the danger passes."

"What if that takes a week? Or a month?"

The idea of living with Brooke in the hotel for a whole month held a certain amount of appeal, especially when he remembered their kiss. Close proximity would certainly lead to more of that. Bracing his arm on the back of the sofa, he leaned over her. "I wouldn't mind."

Her full lips parted. She seemed surprised by his nearness but didn't push him away. "I know how much you like to have everything under your control. But if Jackson Warren is as clever as you say, he'll find a way, no matter where I am."

He refused to acknowledge the truth in that statement. "I won't let that happen."

"I appreciate that, Michael, but I know—from experience—that there's no way to thwart a determined stalker. I had to move halfway across the country to stop Thomas."

She had a point but he persisted with his argument. "Your house isn't safe, and we have to take every precaution we can."

Tension tightened the fine lines at the corners of her eyes. "The real reason I need to go home is emotional."

"How so?"

"I won't live in fear." She lifted her stubborn little chin. "Ever since you told me about Jackson, I haven't been able to sleep well. Even when I'm awake, I'm getting hit with flashes of panic. That's no way to live."

He blamed that bastard of an ex-husband who had done this to her. "You've been through a lot. Any rational human being would be shaken."

"This isn't rational. It's *emotional*."

The irritation in her voice sparked a similar response in him. Her refusal to cooperate was getting under his skin. Yet he would have been a whole lot more annoyed if he hadn't been so close to her—close enough to notice the fine texture of her skin, lightly colored with a pink blush. Desire welled up inside him, and he couldn't fight it. "Let me take care of you."

Reaching up, she placed her hand on his cheek. "I don't expect you to understand what it's like."

He leaned closer to her full, inviting lips. "I know all about danger."

"I'm talking about fear." She slid out from under his scrutiny, scrambling to her feet and facing him. "Being terrified of every shadow. Hearing the sound of footsteps in the whisper of the wind. Living life on the verge of a scream."

"Let me take you to Alabama. To a place where you'll be one hundred percent secure."

"There's nowhere to hide from fear," she said. "I need to reclaim my normal life. That's why it's so important for me to go back to my house. I won't let fear win."

He had to admire her courage. The enemy she fought— fear incarnate—was far more menacing than any real-life combatant. "Okay, I'll take you home."

She rewarded him with a smile. "It's not a reckless decision. You told me that you'd had the locks changed at my house and an alarm system installed." A wider smile. "And you'll be with me."

He hoped those precautions would be enough. "Just in case you change your mind, I'm going to keep this suite."

"But it's so expensive."

"Not a problem," he said. "And while I'm living at your place, I insist on paying half the rent. Don't even think about objecting. I won't hear it."

He scooped up his computer and headed toward the bedroom before she could object. "I have a few details I need to take care of."

He closed the door and stood at the window, looking out at the ski slope. It was nearing the end of the day when the gondola quit running. Snowboarders and skiers were making their last runs.

Michael punched in the number on his cell for his friend—possibly his *former* friend—on the Atlanta police force. He wanted to know why his contact betrayed his confidence.

Detective Harry Rocheford answered on the second ring. "Hey, Michael. Don't you know I'm off duty?"

Michael hoped he'd interrupted Harry's dinner. "At what time does your big mouth go off duty?"

"Come again?"

"When I asked for your opinion about Brooke Johnson, I didn't expect you'd tell her former husband."

After a couple ticks of silence, Harry responded, "I figured Thomas Johnson ought to be informed that Brooke was in danger."

Michael held his anger in check. Until now, Harry had always been helpful in his investigations. "She's not married to him anymore."

"I made a mistake," Harry admitted. "I knew it as soon as I talked to him. He was with his new fiancée, also an attorney. When I mentioned Brooke's name, she started to pull away from him. He yanked her back. His fingers dug into her arm so hard that she winced. And he looked mad. I thought he was about to blow a gasket."

It sounded like Thomas had already started abusing his new girlfriend. If Michael had been in Atlanta, he might have found it necessary to pay Thomas a visit and give him a taste of the fear he so readily afflicted on women. His cruelty had left deep scars on Brooke, and he hated to think that this guy was doing the same thing to someone else.

"A word of advice," Michael drawled. "If this current girlfriend comes to you for a restraining order, you might want to take her seriously."

"I'm inclined to agree with you."

If only the Atlanta PD had taken Brooke seriously. Michael changed the topic. "Are you still keeping an eye on the other jurors?"

"As best I can. Nobody has reported any kind of threat."

"That's a good thing."

"But it don't count as progress. I still haven't seen hide

or hair of any of the suspects you told me to watch for."
He paused. "Kind of surprising. All those Warren boys
have records. I'd expect them to get into trouble. Sooner
than later."

"We'll talk again, Harry."

Michael disconnected the call, watching the shadows
on the ski slope. He knew why Harry Rocheford hadn't
been able to pick up Jackson Warren: because he was right
here in Aspen, planning his next murder.

BROOKE SAT at the desk, checking her e-mails. She found
nothing ominous—just the usual weird messages about
sex toys and investment scams. Tucked in with the junk
mail was a note from her mom that included a recipe for
New England clam chowder.

Brooke knew she ought to keep her mother informed
about what was happening to her. But what could she say?
*Hi, Mom. Everything's fine, except my roommate was
murdered, and I'm the target of a psychopathic killer.
Thanks for the recipe.*

She couldn't expect her sweet, gentle, utterly normal
parents to understand the dark turn her life had taken.
They hadn't raised her to be an abused wife or the target
of a serial murderer. They expected her life to be a series
of happy announcements about getting engaged, getting
married and having babies. Her mother had been delighted
when Brooke's photo appeared on the society page in the
Atlanta newspapers. She never saw the pain behind
Brooke's smile, and Brooke was glad to have spared her
family that. Her divorce had been hard enough on them.

She closed her e-mail and opened her document file, in-
tending to make an entry in her journal. She'd started a
computer diary on the advice of her therapist. Though she

didn't make daily entries, it sometimes helped to write things down. Maybe writing could help her figure out a way to tell her mother about what was happening.

The most recent entry was dated on the day of Sally's death. Brooke noticed two things about it. It was brief. And Brooke hadn't written it.

Bolting from the chair, she backed away from the computer as if it were a rattlesnake coiled to strike. "Michael! Michael, come here!"

He entered the room like a shot. "What is it?"

"My computer. My journal." She pointed at the screen. "Read the last entry."

Squinting, he read aloud, "I can't take the pain anymore. It's time for me to end it. I welcome death. Goodbye."

"That looks like a suicide note," she said.

"And you didn't write it?"

"Absolutely not. I wouldn't use my journal for that. Everything in there is private." And much of it embarrassing. "If I knew I was going to die, my journal is the first thing I'd delete."

"Is your computer password protected?"

"Not when I'm home. I usually just log in and leave it on." The implication of the suicide note sank into her consciousness. "If I'd been killed instead of Sally, the police would have checked all the files on my computer. They would have found this entry and called it proof."

"It's evidence," he said.

"That I was the intended victim. I was supposed to be dead, and this would have been my last statement. You were right, Michael."

She regarded the journal entry with mixed emotions. The suicide note would prove to the FBI and local police that she was the target. But the idea of opening her journal to all those other eyes caused her gut to wrench. "Showing this to someone else would be like turning myself inside out. I never meant for anyone to see it."

She'd detailed her abuse and written out her nightmares as clearly as she could. Some entries were nothing but a string of curses and rants that would never come out of her mouth in public.

Michael turned away from the computer. "There's a problem here. We can't prove that Jackson wrote that note."

"Who else could have?"

"You."

"But I didn't write it," she said, confused.

"I know that because I know you." He frowned. "But the feds and Deputy McGraw don't share my insight. They might look at this journal entry and think you're trying to set them up, trying to get attention."

"Like the police in Atlanta." Thomas had convinced them that her complaints were nonsense, that she was nothing but a hysterical woman. "What should we do?"

"Accept that journal entry as proof of our theory. There's no need to have your computer dusted for prints. None of Jackson's fingerprints turned up in the rest of the house, so we can assume he was wearing gloves. There's no good reason to show your journal to the police."

She dropped into the chair and shut down her computer. *No need to make all my crazy ramblings public. Thank God.* The tension coiled inside her began to unwind, and she felt a strange sense of relief. Proof of a serial killer should *not* feel good, but there was very little left in her life that made any sense. Her world had turned upside down and was spinning out of control.

She rose from her chair and faced Michael. "Thank you."

He accepted her gratitude with a nod. "I don't suppose this suicide note changes your mind about staying here at the hotel."

"Not a bit."

As she looked at the handsome man in front of her, she found herself hoping that when they got to her house he wouldn't feel obliged to sleep in Sally's room. She decided she wouldn't mind at all if he protected her body from a very close position—maybe right beside her in bed.

She kept her desire to herself as Michael packed some of his clothes. No matter what happened, he would always be well-groomed with his brown hair neatly combed and his shirt tucked in. He was a true Southern gent—a man who paid attention to his appearance. She liked that.

When he said they'd be taking his rental car, she didn't argue at all, even though she would have liked to take her own car. Tomorrow, they'd be back in town so she could go to work, and she could pick up her car then.

And Michael was proud of his new choice in rental car: a shiny, black Hummer. These heavy-duty vehicles weren't all that unusual in Aspen, but she still felt conspicuous, as if they ought to be part of a military convoy.

During the drive, she found herself looking at him, noticing the jut of his chin and his high cheekbones. At first glance, his jade eyes dominated his very masculine face, but his other features were equally appealing. And when he smiled, he was devastatingly handsome.

When they arrived at her house, she was so happy to be home, she was almost cheerful. He parked the Hummer near the back door and turned to her.

"Here's your new key," he said. "One for you and one for me. I'm going to open the door right now to show you how the alarm system operates."

"Is it one of those keypad things?"

"It's not that complicated. I wanted something top-of-the-line with all the bells and whistles, but the technician said he'd have to re-wire your whole house to install a system that rang through to a security company. If you lived in the elite area of Aspen, it wouldn't be a problem. But your A-frame is too isolated."

"It took forever for the police to respond to my 911 call."

"Exactly," he said. "By the time a security guard got to your house, it'd be too late."

She took her key chain from her backpack and added the new key. "How does this system work?"

"Sensors in the windows and doors. If anybody tries to break in, an alarm starts screaming. Kind of like a car alarm."

"What if it goes off when we're not here?"

"Your nearest neighbor is at least a mile away," he pointed out. "Not that I care about disturbing them or upsetting the local chipmunk population. Our safety is my priority. When we leave, the system stays on. That way we won't find any nasty surprises waiting for us."

She followed him to the door and watched as he slid the key into the new, shiny lock. When he stepped inside, he used the same key on a metal pad above the light switch.

"Deactivated," he said. "To turn it on, turn the key in the opposite direction."

"Got it."

It felt good to be home. She glanced around the kitchen, noticing that the cleaning crew had done a good job. All the dishes and glasses were put away, and the countertops gleamed. The front room was swept, vacuumed and dusted. Logs for a fire had been arranged in the stone fireplace.

Though it would be a long time before she could walk past the place where Sally's body had been hanging without a shiver of horror, she steadily made her way past the spot and headed to the sliding glass doors.

The edge of nightfall. This was almost the same time she'd come home two days ago to find her roommate murdered. She flicked the switch beside the doors and the outdoor lights illuminated the deck outside. If these lights had been on that night, she would have been able to clearly see the intruder and could have saved herself a ton of self-doubt. "I think I'll leave these lights on."

"Good plan," Michael said. "Also the light over the back door. A simple precaution that helps to keep intruders away."

"I'm beginning to think that I did see him." Her fingertips touched the cold glass. "Jackson Warren was just this close. If you hadn't shown up when you did, I'd probably be dead."

"Much as I'd like to take credit, I'm not so sure. It's important to him to get away with his crime, to make it look like your death is an accident."

"Or a suicide."

She pushed those ominous thoughts away as they headed upstairs and got settled. Michael went to Sally's bedroom where her personal belongings were neatly boxed up and waiting to be removed. Brooke's bedroom was tidy and clean, just the way she liked it.

When she'd first moved into this house, it felt like a sanctuary. Those feelings began to return as she brewed some tea and lit the logs in the fireplace. With these simple tasks, she was reclaiming her home.

While she sat beside Michael in front of the fireplace, they talked about anything and everything. For the first time since they'd met, she was able to focus on the man separate from all that had happened. The many layers of Michael Shaw intrigued her. He reminisced about his rough-and-tumble life in the Marine Corps, then recounted the life experiences of a sophisticated man who sat on the board of a biotech company. Worldly and down-home at the same time, he appreciated the finer things in life—but also liked to get down and dirty. He was the kind of guy who might go to a monster truck rally in the afternoon and the opera at night.

A sense of comfort wrapped around her like a soft down comforter. Tonight, she knew, her sleep would be untroubled.

When the time came to climb the staircase and retire to their separate bedrooms, she toyed with the idea of inviting him to join her.

But not tonight. For now, it was enough to get a good night's sleep, resting secure in the knowledge that he was nearby to protect her.

At approximately four in the morning, the alarm sounded.

Chapter Eleven

Michael shot out of bed, grabbed his gun from the night-stand and raced to Brooke's bedroom. He hit the switch for the overhead light and found her sitting up on the bed with the covers pulled up to her neck.

"Are you all right?" he shouted over the harsh scream of the alarm.

"Yes," she yelled back.

"Go to the bathroom," he ordered. "Lock the door, and get in the tub."

"Why?"

"Just do it." There wasn't time to explain that the bathtub provided a shell of protection in case bullets started flying—and Brooke probably wouldn't want to hear that right now anyway. Calling 911 was pointless. By the time the sheriff got here, they'd both be dead and their attacker long gone.

He stepped onto the balcony overlooking the front room. The lights on the deck outside the sliding glass doors showed that the doors were still locked and the windows unbroken. The only other points of entry were the kitchen windows and the back door.

If the alarm had been tripped by an armed intruder,

Michael knew he'd be an easy target as he descended the staircase leading to the main floor. But there wasn't any other route.

The alarm continued to scream.

He looked over his shoulder and saw Brooke in the bathroom doorway. "Go inside, Brooke! Lock the door!"

The last thing he needed was to be distracted by having her in the line of fire. He edged along the banister toward the staircase. His strategy was unabated assault—that was the only option available to him. He would fly down the stairs and into the kitchen without pause, not allowing his opponent to think or take aim. Most people were so stunned when confronted like that by a berserk Marine that they backed down.

Barefoot, he charged down the stairs and ran full out toward the wall separating the kitchen. A battle cry rose in his throat. Like a screaming eagle, he hurtled through the doorway. And found no one.

None of the windows were broken. The kitchen door was still locked.

He made a rapid search using only the ambient light from outside. No interior light. If a sniper waited outside, Michael wasn't about to provide illumination for a clear shot.

He found nothing out of place.

Using an extra key they'd hidden in a kitchen drawer, he turned off the alarm. In the sudden silence that blanketed the house, he could hear the thudding of his own heartbeat as adrenaline coursed through his veins.

He exhaled a long, slow breath. The problem with a sensor alarm system was that anything touching the window or door could set it off. It might have been nothing more than a bird hopping on a windowsill, but he still wanted to investigate outside.

"Michael?" Brooke called down from upstairs. "Is it safe?"

It was clear that he needed to have a little chat with Brooke about how to react in emergencies. She shouldn't have left the bathtub without his okay. Her job was to follow his orders without asking questions.

"Michael?"

"It's okay," he called out.

Before he checked the perimeter of the house, he needed more protection from the cold. All he had on was a pair of sweatpants—a lack of preparedness that was unforgivable. If he'd seen someone outside the windows, he wouldn't have been able to pursue with any efficiency. He certainly wouldn't have gotten far without shoes in the snow.

Brooke entered the kitchen. Like him, she was wearing only her night clothes. Half of his brain noticed how sexy she looked even in a knee-length, red-and-white striped shirt—and the other half wanted to yell at her for failing to follow orders.

"I need a gun," she said.

His first instinct was to refuse her request. Putting a firearm in the hands of someone who didn't know how to use it was dangerous. "Let's go back upstairs and get dressed."

"Can I turn on a light?"

"No. Upstairs. Now."

After rearming the alarm, he followed her up the staircase and herded her into her bedroom. "Was it a false alarm?" she asked.

"Nobody broke into the house. Nothing was out of place. But I'm still going to take a look outside to make sure we're not in any danger."

"I'll come with you," she said.

Since when had she become so bold? This was a woman who—by her own admission—lived her life in fear. "You're not scared?"

She frowned as she considered. "Apparently not. That's strange, isn't it?"

"Not really." As she paced away from him and pivoted, his gaze fixed on her bare legs and the way her hips moved inside her striped nightshirt.

"I know what it is," she said. "A direct threat doesn't scare me because there's something I can do about it."

"Right now, Brooke, I'd prefer if you'd stay inside with your cell phone. If a problem should arise while I'm outside, keep the doors locked and call for backup."

"This is why I need a gun of my own. If something happens to you, I'm on my own."

Though he still wasn't happy about the idea of arming Brooke, she made a good point. "I'll look into it tomorrow. I should also pick up some night goggles. And maybe a long-range rifle."

"Sounds like we're getting ready for war."

"A battle." And he was more than ready to finally confront Jackson Warren. "I should get dressed."

She was looking at his chest as if she'd just noticed that he was half-naked. A grin teased the corners of her mouth. "Do you have to? Get dressed?"

The adrenaline still pulsing in his veins urged him to take action, to pull her into his arms and kiss that grin off her delectable lips. But he needed to check outside. His mission to keep her safe came first.

WRAPPED IN her bathrobe with cell phone in hand, Brooke watched through the kitchen window as Michael prowled outside the house. Though he'd taken a flashlight, she didn't see the beam. He moved stealthily away from the circle of light near the door and headed up the side of the snow-covered cliff. She lost sight of him amidst the overhanging tree branches and outcroppings of rocks that were familiar in daylight but ominous in night's shadows. Michael had vanished.

Not for long, she hoped. If he hadn't been here, her burst of courage would have been nothing more than a pop and a fizzle. Though she'd told him her unexpected bravery came from facing a tangible threat, the truth was that she drew strength from Michael's presence. He made her want to forget the past and move forward. He'd promised to keep her safe, and she trusted him.

Where was he? Her fingers hovered above the keys on her cell phone, ready to punch in 911. Seconds ticked by. How long should she wait? One minute? Five? Ten?

She opened the door a crack, ignoring the cold, and listened, hearing only the small sounds of nature: the quiet fall of a pinecone, the rustling of nocturnal creatures, the hiss of wind.

Then loud footfalls crunched through the snow. Michael tromped into the light.

She yanked the door wide open. "Where were you?"

"Checking the hillside." He turned on his flashlight. "I'm going to circle the house and look for footprints. I'll only be a couple of minutes."

She hesitated in the doorway, so relieved to see him that she wanted to dash across the snow and swan dive into his arms. When he was running through the house earlier wearing only sweatpants, she'd gotten a nice, long look at his muscled chest and lean torso. A very impressive view. In spite of the danger of that moment, in spite of the gun in his hand, she was wondering how it would feel to run her hands across his chest and press her body tightly against his.

Closing the door, she went to the small kitchen table and sat. She couldn't believe that she'd been watching Michael's gorgeous body while her alarm system was going off. She could feel the awakening of long repressed desire when she looked at him. Her instincts told her that making love with Michael would be better than anything she'd ever experienced before. Should she? Would it just make everything more confusing?

Looking down at the cell phone, she saw that she had a message. After the phone call from Thomas, she'd turned it off. The only call she'd made today was to Hannah, informing her that she'd be at the shop tomorrow.

There was a message from Tammy Gallegos thanking them for stopping by and promising to be careful. Brooke was glad that Tammy would be leaving the country and would be far away from any threat from Jackson Warren.

Michael entered through the back door and stamped his feet. "I need better boots. My toes are frostbit."

"You flatlanders are all alike," she teased. "Can't take a little mountain chill."

"It must be zero degrees out there."

Should she offer to share her bodily warmth with him in her bed? The invitation was on the tip of her tongue, but she held back. Instead, she cleared her throat and said, "Did you find anything outside?"

"There are too many footprints leading up to the back door from the locksmith and the cleaning crew." He peeled off his gloves and shoved them into the pocket of his jacket before taking it off. "Somebody might have set off the alarm by jiggling the doorknob, but there's no way to know."

"Another threat that can't be proved." She looked at her phone, glad that she hadn't summoned the sheriff. "Why did you think somebody might be up on the hill?"

He hung his jacket on a peg by the door. "Setting off the alarm could have been a ruse to draw us outside where we'd be easy targets for a sniper."

"Sniper!" she yelped. That possibility had never crossed her mind.

"Your A-frame is pretty well-protected. The windows at the front open onto a view of the opposite side of the canyon. The bedroom windows aren't accessible to a sniper. There are only these two kitchen windows and not many places where a shooter could get a good angle."

Her thoughts of passion faded as she imagined a sharp-shooter crouched on the hillside, hiding amid trees and shadows. "But that's not Jackson's style."

"It's not," Michael agreed as he blew on his hands to warm them. "He wants to commit murder in a way that won't have the feds breathing down his neck. Still, I like to consider all the angles."

"You're good at this."

"With police training and Marine Corps battle experience, I wouldn't be bragging to say that I'm a top-notch bodyguard."

"I guess I'm lucky to have you guarding my body."

He turned and cast a steady, smoldering gaze in her direction. "You have a fine body, Brooke. It'd be a shame if anything happened to it."

The intense green of his eyes enticed her, and she knew that the slightest hint of compliance from her would lead them upstairs to share her bed. She was tempted, deeply tempted.

But she wasn't ready. Not yet. Glancing at the wall

clock, she said, "It's coming up on five. Hardly seems worth it to go back to bed."

"Your decision," he said. "If you want to go to bed—"

"I should try to get a bit more sleep." She stood. "I need to work tomorrow. Good night, Michael. And thank you."

Avoiding his seductive gaze, she maneuvered around him and rushed up the staircase. She closed her bedroom door and leaned against it, her heart beating fast. Falling asleep was pretty much out of the question. Usually she couldn't sleep because she was terrified. Tonight was different—fear played no part in her wakefulness. She was excited and aroused, both feelings she had not experienced in a very long time.

Stretched out on her bed, she tried to read until the skies outside her bedroom window began to lighten. A new day. Another day with Michael as her protector.

The aroma of fresh brewed coffee greeted her when she went down to the kitchen after her shower. Michael sat at the table scribbling notes on a piece of paper. When he looked up and gave her a lazy smile, her heart took a little leap, and she felt a hot flush working its way up her neck. There was something so intimate about sharing the morning hours.

"I'm making a shopping list," he said. "So far, I've got handgun, night goggles, boots and eggs. There's not much in your fridge other than beer."

"That belonged to Sally."

The freezer contained a loaf of bread, which she took out. "We can have toast."

Obviously dissatisfied, he made a grumbling noise in the back of his throat.

She opened a kitchen cabinet. "I have canned goods."

"I'm not a picky eater," he drawled, "but I draw the line at baked beans and peanut butter for breakfast."

"We'll go to the supermarket." She poured herself a mug of coffee, placed it on the table and sat opposite him. "I'll bet you're a meat and potatoes kind of guy."

"Because I hail from the South? That's not a fair stereotype. Though I do like my food breaded and deep-fried."

She added her three spoonfuls of sugar from the container on the table. "Let me make the grocery list. I like to cook."

There was something especially appealing about the idea of preparing meals for Michael. She ran through several alternatives in her head. Lemon chicken. A brisket stew. Steak béarnaise with mushrooms.

With her mouth beginning to water, she sipped her sweetened coffee. "That was a joke about the deep-fried stuff, right?"

"Right," he said. "I might be from Alabama, but I don't require pan gravy with every meal." He gave her a wink and headed upstairs.

While he showered, she took the list he'd started and added several items. She made a note to get fresh coffee beans. This brew tasted a bit stale, but it didn't matter—the real point to morning coffee was caffeine. Having it taste good was merely a bonus.

While trying to decide on items for the list, she doodled on the page. A little daisy with nine petals. And teeth. She laughed. No teeth. She loved daisies.

There was the L-word. Might be dangerous to even think it in any context right now. She set down her pen and finished her coffee. Love could be such a strange thing. She tried to remember the exact moment when she knew she didn't love Thomas. It had happened years ago, long before she'd ever thought of divorce. Maybe after her miscarriage.

She'd been two months and three weeks pregnant and knew her baby was a boy. Trevor. She'd wanted to name him Trevor. When he died, Thomas refused to bury an empty coffin. But she needed to mourn, needed a marker.

Vividly, she remembered a hot, humid weekend in June, two years ago. Though Colorado snow blanketed the hillside outside her window, she felt the Georgia heat. In her mind, she saw the lush green foliage and heard the hum of insects. She'd gone to a campground by herself and burned the blue blanket and the baby clothes she'd purchased for Trevor.

She recalled how soft those little shirts were and the feel of the satin edge on the blanket. Those were the ashes she scattered. Alone, in the verdant Georgia forests where the trees were as tall as skyscrapers, she wished her unborn son Godspeed.

"Trevor," she whispered. Usually she tried not to think of his name, much less speak it. Why had she gone down this path? Why was her memory so painfully clear?

She reached for the pen, but her fingers were too clumsy. After three tries, she managed to balance the pen. Writing was impossible. She could only manage a scribble. *What is wrong with me?*

Probably a lack of sleep. *I need to move around.* She pushed away from the table and stood. Through her feet were on the floor, the room seemed to be moving, rotating slowly. Or was she turning around?

Her stomach wrenched.

She knew this sickness. The clumsiness. The spinning. The pain. She'd been drugged.

Chapter Twelve

Drugs—prescription or otherwise—were poison to her system. Brooke had learned about her low tolerance when her therapist suggested antianxiety and depression drugs. Nothing agreed with her, not even in minimal dosage. She'd had delusions. And pain. Just like now.

The pressure on her gut intensified. But she hadn't taken a pill. She hadn't even eaten anything. Just coffee. Sweat beaded on her forehead. Miserable, she felt miserable. It couldn't have been the coffee because Michael was drinking it.

The sugar. Her three spoonfuls of sugar.

Poison.

The edges of her vision darkened. She knew what came next. Vertigo. Dizziness. Then hallucination.

She had to rid herself of this sickness.

Staggering, she lurched to the sink and vomited. Turning the tap on, she washed the disgusting miasma down the drain and turned on the garbage disposal.

The pain stabbed harder. She had to get every bit of this poison out of her system before her gut was devoured from the inside. Her eyes were already affected—she saw jagged prisms at the edge of her peripheral vision. They snapped at her like rows of giant shark teeth.

Putting her finger down her throat, she forced herself to gag. Nothing came up. Dry heaves.

In disjointed moves, she grabbed a glass from the cabinet and added salt. The back of her throat ached, but she forced herself to drink. One full glass. Then another. Halfway through the third glass, her gag reflex kicked in. She leaned over the sink, vomiting again.

As if from faraway, she heard Michael's voice, felt his hands on her shoulders.

"Drugs," she croaked. "I was drugged."

She felt him pulling her away from the sink. "I'll take you to the hospital."

"No." That was one thing she would not do. "No hospital."

"Brooke, you're not thinking straight. Let me—"

"I said no." She struggled to prepare another glass of salted water. The cure was to vomit, to clear her system. Again, she leaned over the sink.

Was this enough? It had to be enough. Exhaustion sapped her strength. Her knees buckled.

Before she hit the floor, Michael caught her. His arms wrapped around her waist, holding her upright. Once again, he wanted to control the situation. But she wouldn't allow it.

"No hospital," she said with as much force as she could muster. "No doctors."

"What can I do to help?" he asked.

"Upstairs."

As he carried her through the house, she pressed her hands against her belly. The pain had subsided to a persistent throb, but her body was burning up. More exhausted than if she'd run a marathon, she clung to consciousness. Sweat soaked through her clothes.

Though she couldn't remember how he maneuvered her up the narrow staircase, they were in the upstairs bathroom. She was alert enough to be aware of her surroundings and embarrassed by her sickness. No one should have to see her like this, especially not Michael.

"Put me down," she said. When he released her, she braced herself on the sink and pulled open the medicine cabinet. "You can go now."

"Not a chance," he said. "What are you looking for?"

"Ipecac."

He found the bottle, removed the top and handed it to her.

She took a swig. "I need a glass for water. Get it for me?"

As soon as he left the bathroom, another wave of nausea churned through her. She crumpled to the floor. Threw up in the toilet.

Fighting back sobs, she looked around. The room held steady. But the tiles on the floor and the baseboard wavered at the edge of hallucination. She felt like hell.

When Michael returned with the water glass, she took another shot of ipecac and downed the water. "Leave me, Michael."

"I'm staying right here."

"Don't need you. Not now." And she didn't want him to see her puking. "I have this under control."

"You said you'd been drugged."

"Must have been something in the sugar." Bile rose in her throat. The back of her mouth tasted like rotting garbage. "I have a low tolerance for drugs."

"This has happened to you before?"

"Yes." She fought the urge to vomit. "Get out. Please."

"That's why you have ipecac in your medicine cabinet."

"Enough questions." She pressed her lips together. "Leave, please leave."

As soon as he stepped into the hallway, she leaned over the toilet again.

Whatever drug had infiltrated her body must be gone by now, assuming she'd acted quickly enough. If she had, her home remedy was at least as effective as a stomach pump. She was drained. Literally, drained. At this point, the greatest danger was dehydration.

Fearing the worst, she checked her reflection in the bathroom mirror. A sickly white sheen coated her skin. Her hair was matted. Less than an hour ago, she'd been on top of the world. Now she looked like something that had crawled from the depths.

Michael's handsome and very serious face appeared beside her in the mirror. "I want to take you to the hospital. You should be hooked up to a saline solution."

"I won't go."

"If not for yourself, do it for me. I'd feel better if I knew you were getting the best of care."

Reaching out, he gently stroked her back. Earlier today, she'd been longing for his touch. But not like this.

A surge of purpose gave her strength. "I don't need medical attention."

"What do you have against doctors?"

"Do you have any idea what happens to people who show up at the hospital with a drug overdose? Even an accidental overdose? Everyone assumes it was a suicide attempt. When this happened to me before…"

She shuddered at the memory. Waking in her hospital bed, she'd found herself restrained so she wouldn't try to hurt herself. Tied down and helpless, she had struggled to convince the doctors that she wasn't crazy. It wasn't their fault; they were only doing their jobs. But she'd vowed to never again endure that sort of intense, pitying scrutiny. Never again.

"There are procedures for suicidal patients. I had to fight to be released."

"I understand," he said quietly. "Sometimes the hospital files a police report."

Of course, he'd know. He was a cop.

MICHAEL UNDERSTOOD her reluctance to be admitted to a hospital, but he wasn't entirely comfortable with self-treatment, especially since she'd be depending on him to take care of her. Feeding her chicken soup? Soothing her fevered brow with a damp cloth? Not his thing. He'd rather fight off twenty armed assailants. At least he knew how to do that.

He paced the length of the balcony while she got into the shower. Okay, his job was to play nursemaid. What should he do? As soon as he heard water running, he poked his head into the bathroom. "Brooke? How are you doing?"

"I think I'll survive. Barely."

Given the intensity of her sickness, he wasn't able to find that funny. "Do you have any idea what kind of drug you ingested?"

Over the sound of the shower, she said, "It wasn't anything caustic, like a poison. I would have tasted that. The sensations reminded me of an antidepressant. Aching stomach. Woozy head."

"Do you have anything like that in the house?"

"Absolutely not. After I went this route with my therapist, I never take anything stronger than aspirin."

Her violent reaction to the drugs had probably saved her life. If she hadn't started vomiting, she might have slipped into unconsciousness. By the time he'd figured out what was wrong with her, it would have been too late.

"Michael? How do you think this happened?"

"With the cleaning crew and the locksmith, there were a lot of people coming and going. Somebody could have slipped inside and doctored the sugar in the container on the table."

"Somebody?" Inside the shower, her voice echoed with bitterness. "Somebody like Stonewall Jackson Warren."

If she had OD'd, her death would have looked like she killed herself, backed up by the suicide note on her computer, even if they assumed she'd written the note several days before she took her life. The cops and the feds would have written her off, and Jackson would have moved on to his next victim.

He sat on the closed toilet seat and stared at the shower curtain, feeling useless and uncertain. "Is there anything I can do?"

"I need to rehydrate gradually," she said. "There's water with electrolytes in the fridge. It's supposed to absorb better."

"I'm getting it."

In the kitchen, he glanced at the list she'd started. Giant flower doodles all but blanked out the words, which wasn't really a problem because he doubted they'd be leaving the house for the rest of today. Brooke needed time to recuperate.

Returning to the upstairs balcony, he saw her leaving the bathroom, wearing nothing but a burgundy towel. Her wet hair tangled around her face in sopping strands. Her pale skin gleamed. Her arms and shoulders were graceful and feminine.

He was stunned by the sight of her. Before he could censor himself, he said, "You're beautiful."

With a weak smile, she said, "I've looked better."

He stood, unable to take his eyes off her. "What can I do? Should I carry you to your room?"

"I'll manage." She moved the few steps toward her bedroom door. "Let me get changed back into my night-shirt."

"I can help," he offered.

"I bet you can."

She closed the bedroom door. This was the story of their relationship. One closed door after another. He was growing tried of waiting for her to invite him inside. He knew he wanted him on some level. Sometimes he caught her looking at him with fire in her eyes. Each time they touched, it was electric. And there had been that kiss.

Unfortunately, now was not the time for thoughts of intimacy. The woman had just survived another murder attempt.

Michael needed to be patient, to wait for the right time. When he first started dating, his Uncle Elmo gave him a piece of advice: A woman is like a hunting dog. She might be wagging her tail and giving you sloppy kisses, but her real purpose is the hunt. When she's ready, you'll know. Good old Uncle Elmo.

That moment—their moment—would come. Sooner rather than later, he hoped.

She opened the bedroom door, her bathrobe wrapped around her. "I'm cold. I think I should go back to bed."

"You might still have drugs in your system, Brooke. It wouldn't be good to fall asleep."

"You're right." She looked tired. "Maybe I should go sit by the fire."

Starting a fire would give him something to do instead of hovering around like a useless bystander. "Lean on me. I'll help you down the stairs."

When he wrapped his arm around her slender waist, he smelled the clean fragrance of soap and shampoo. Her body rubbed against his as they moved slowly toward the staircase. She was weak. Her hands trembled as she clung to him. When they made it down the stairs, she collapsed onto the small sofa in front of the fireplace.

He did everything he could to make her comfortable. Built a fire. Fetched her slippers and a blanket to keep her warm. Provided her with two bottles of electrolyte water.

"Anything else?" he asked.

"My hair." She plucked at a damp strand. "I should go back upstairs to the bathroom and use the blow-dryer. Otherwise it's going to be a disaster."

"You stay here. I'll take care of it."

He charged back up the staircase to the bathroom. Her hair dryer required an outlet, which meant he'd need a really long extension cord for it to work on the sofa near the fireplace. He grabbed her brush and comb. Though he didn't have a clue about how to style hair, he'd give it try.

Back downstairs, he watched her take a small sip of the water. "How's your stomach?"

She held up the water bottle and tried to gauge how much she'd imbibed. "Half gone. And I haven't gagged."

"That's progress. Want to try a piece of toast?"

Slowly, she shook her head from side to side. Her eyelids drooped. She was so pale that her skin seemed translucent.

He pulled a rocking chair closer to the sofa and held up the wide-toothed comb like a maestro about to conduct an orchestra. "Hold still."

She eyed him suspiciously. "What are you doing?"

"Fixing your hair."

"I can do it." She reached for the comb.

"You need to rest. Concentrate on taking in liquid."

Too tired to argue, she sat quietly as he stroked the comb from the top of her scalp to her nape. Being careful not to tug, he separated the tangles and smoothed her hair down to her shoulders. He twisted a curl around his finger. Never in his life had he done anything like this.

"When we go into town," she said in a quiet voice, "we should take the sugar to Deputy McGraw. He could have it analyzed. If he finds drugs, that would be proof…" Her words faded. "Proof that someone tried to kill me."

"Not necessarily." Lifting the hair away from her ears, he raked the comb to the ends.

"Why not?"

"Unless someone witnessed Jackson putting drugs into the sugar, it's not proof. Anyone could have done it," he said. "The feds would probably say I did it. Doctored the sugar to prove my case about a serial killer."

"Or me." She exhaled a sigh. "Because I'm crazy and suicidal."

"Uh-huh." With his fingers, he pulled the hair away from her face.

"Feels good," she murmured.

"Like this?" Starting at her temples, he used his fingers to knead her scalp.

A contented groan escaped her lips. "That's wonderful."

"You like massages?"

"Who doesn't?"

Now he had a mission. When he finished with her hair, he went to the other end of the sofa, took off her slippers and massaged the curve of her arch, the turn of her slender ankle and each pink toe.

She'd liked when he caressed her head, but a foot massage seemed to be pure ecstasy. Her sighs and moans of pleasure were driving him crazy. He could do this for her the rest of the day—easy.

When he'd finished with her feet, she sat up straighter on the sofa. "That was good."

He longed to peel off her bathrobe and extend the massage to her entire body. "Do you want more?"

"I should try to eat something." She tipped the water bottle to her lips. "If I can keep toast down, I still want to go into town today."

"You need time to recover."

"I don't plan to put in a full day at work." She looked better. A bit of color had returned to her cheeks. "I had a thought. We could print copies of the Jackson Warren photo on your computer, and I could give one to Hannah. If he came into the shop, she'd be able to identify him."

"Good idea." He could also give a photo to Deputy McGraw. "But we don't have to do anything today. There's no need to rush."

Her focus sharpened. "He tried to kill me, Michael. I don't want to wait around for his next attempt. Do you?"

No. No, he definitely did not.

Chapter Thirteen

They left the house around noon. Since Brooke insisted that she was fine and needed things from town—specifically her own handgun—Michael agreed to go forward with the day's plans. His preference would have been to spend the rest of the day on that full-body massage he'd started, but he understood her need to take action. Though less talkative than usual, she kept a smile on her face as she gazed through the windshield at the winter sunlight glistening on the snow.

For a moment, he considered telling her that the color of her eyes matched the radiant blue of the skies. Her hair—without the benefit of a blow-dryer—fluffed around her face in shining auburn waves that begged for his touch. But he held back on his compliments.

In town, the number of people milling around and riding the Silver Queen gondola had increased, probably because it was a Friday during ski season. The boutique had a lot of foot traffic, which Michael considered a plus. He felt safe leaving her there. Jackson wouldn't attack in front of witnesses—an obvious murder would garner too much attention.

Michael went to the courthouse where he'd arranged to

meet McGraw. The husky, mustached deputy sat behind his desk eating a sack lunch. He jabbed a carrot stick in Michael's direction. "You see this? My wife thinks carrots and celery count as dessert. If we didn't have muffins in the break room, I'd starve to death."

"I bet she tells you that she's got your best interests at heart. She's keeping an eye on your cholesterol."

"I hate that word. Cholesterol." His deep voice grated like a cement mixer. "What can I do for you, Michael?"

"Any progress on the Sally Klinger case?"

"Not much." McGraw shot him a scowl. "I hear you've been doing some investigating on your own. You paid a visit to Sally's husband in Denver."

Michael understood the hostility. If he'd been in charge of this investigation, he wouldn't have appreciated an outsider making inquiries, either. McGraw was justified in being ticked off about the interference, but Michael wanted to mend that rift. Having the deputy on his side would be invaluable.

"I didn't mean to overstep." Michael set his briefcase on the floor and took a seat on the opposite side of the desk. "That's why I wanted to see you in person. Brooke and I have turned up a couple of clues."

McGraw took a bite of carrot. "Go on."

Michael placed a sealed plastic bag containing the envelope Sally had prepared for her husband on his desk. "Brooke found this envelope in the pocket of her jacket, which Sally borrowed. There's a check inside for a thousand dollars. Written from Sally to her husband, Damien Klinger."

McGraw picked up the envelope and glared at it. "Brooke found this at the house?"

"That's right."

The frown lines across his forehead deepened. "Apparently, my men didn't do a thorough job of checking for evidence."

Michael didn't patronize the deputy with false assurances that they'd done the best they could. His men had missed a clue. It happened. "You called in the Colorado Bureau of Investigation. Have they taken over?"

"CBI is using our facilities for questioning but shipping all the evidence back to Denver for analysis. They don't think much of our forensics."

"Jurisdiction can be a pain in the rear."

"I don't see CBI doing such a good job. They haven't even gotten autopsy results yet." He dropped the plastic bag on his desk. "Did you ask Damien Klinger about this check?"

"He said Sally was paying him back for a car loan."

"Do you believe him?"

"I do." Michael leaned back in his chair. "Usually, I'm the first person to serve up the spouse as a suspect, especially when there's bad blood between husband and wife. But I think Damien Klinger moved on with his life and didn't much care what Sally did."

"The CBI investigators concur with your opinion. Damien Klinger's alibi is considered viable."

Michael remembered Damien's girlfriend—the sweet, straightforward schoolteacher—who had vouched for his whereabouts. "Sally's husband had one interesting observation. He said that if Sally was paying him back, she must have come into money. Probably from a wealthy boyfriend."

"Like Tyler Hennessey." McGraw chomped another bite of carrot and studied Michael. "I shouldn't be talking to you."

"I understand. Back in Birmingham, I'm a detective. Here, I'm a citizen. However, as you well know, I have my own agenda when it comes to this crime. The feds don't believe there's a serial killer, but I do. And he's coming after Brooke."

"Have you got evidence?"

"A suicide note," Michael said. "There was an entry in Brooke's computer journal that she didn't make."

"That she *claims* she didn't make," McGraw corrected. "Is there any way to prove she didn't write it?"

"No." Which was what made Jackson Warren's scheme so diabolical. "But she's not suicidal. Brooke Johnson is a survivor. A fighter."

Though McGraw said nothing, he gave a nod—a small indication that he didn't think Brooke was crazy.

"I've gotten to know her," Michael said. "She takes three spoonfuls of sugar in her coffee. Don't ask me why, but that's her habit. Three spoonfuls."

McGraw leaned forward, showing interest. Michael continued. "All she had to eat this morning was coffee. She ingested something that made her sick. Possibly some kind of drug."

"Somebody doctored the sugar," McGraw said.

Michael opened his briefcase and took out the sugar container, also encased in plastic to preserve any possible fingerprints. He placed it on the desk. "I don't have any right to ask for your help, but I'd appreciate if your forensics people could do an analysis."

The deputy's eyes narrowed as he stared at the clear plastic container. Michael could guess what was going through his head. Though McGraw had willingly called in the CBI and the feds, having them take over the case had hurt his pride. No lawman liked to be dismissed from the scene of the crime.

"You know," McGraw rumbled, "nobody believes your theory about a serial killer."

"I'm aware."

Michael watched as the deputy came to a decision. The scowl lifted. Below his mustache, his mouth curved in a smile as he reached across his desk and pulled the sugar container closer. "I don't see any harm in running a few tests."

Michael gave a quick grin to acknowledge their unspoken complicity. If his theory proved to be correct and McGraw had supported him, the Pitkin County deputy would have outsmarted the feds and CBI. A definite coup.

"Another thing," Michael said. "This is a mug shot for Stonewall Jackson Warren. If you happen to see him—"

"I'll know what to do." McGraw studied the photo. "By the way, you might be interested in knowing that Sally recently deposited five thousand in cash to her bank account."

"Very interested," Michael said.

"She and Tyler Hennessey were on the outs. He told us that Sally had herself a new boyfriend. Not a local, so Tyler didn't know his name. It's hard to pin down an identification—during ski season, Aspen is a town full of strangers."

All of them concealed under parkas, scarves, hats and gloves. A mountain resort was the perfect place for a killer to go unnoticed.

THOUGH BROOKE had only managed to put in four hours of work, she was proud of herself. Instead of spending the day lying around being sick, she'd rallied and coped, which was definitely not the attitude of a suicidal loser. She felt strong. Maybe a bit queasy, but strong.

As she and Michael drove back toward her house, she turned toward him. "Did you remember the mushrooms?"

He shook his head. "I'm not a big fan of edible fungus."

"I should have gone with you to the grocery store. What did you get?"

"Are you feeling hungry?" he asked.

She checked in with her stomach. Throughout the day she'd been eating little bites—a couple of crackers, a bite of apple, a half cup of soup. She hadn't vomited, but her digestive system was still shaky. "I could handle pasta."

"That's what I figured. We're going bland tonight. Nothing deep-fried. Nothing spicy."

"Are you cooking?"

"You don't need to sound so shocked. I've been a bachelor for a long time. I know how to put together a decent dinner."

She didn't quite believe him. Michael was more likely to be served than to do the serving. Suspicious, she asked, "Who taught you?"

"Not my mama, that's for sure. In Mama's house, chores were assigned by gender. Ladies made the supper. Gents took out the garbage. Cooking wasn't considered manly."

She scoffed. "In spite of all those famous chefs who are men?"

"I didn't say Mama made sense." He shrugged. "That's just how it was. After I was on my own, I realized that my options were to live on pizza and burgers or learn to cook. I called my sister, and she was tickled to give me a crash course in the basics of food preparation. She gave me a cookbook and an apron—pink, with ruffles."

"Were you unmanned?"

"Mama considers my skill in the kitchen to be one of the primary reasons I never married."

Brooke laughed. She was familiar with this old-fashioned

mind-set. Her own mother had prepared her to be a full-time chef and housekeeper. "When I was growing up, my specialty was birthday cakes. I loved the decorating part. The family scrapbook is full of pictures of me at varying ages with strange, multicolored designs. For a while, I seemed to be fixated on black and yellow bees."

"Happy Bee Day," he said.

"Clever, huh?"

He gave her a smile and turned his attention back to the road. The more time she spent with Michael, the closer they got. A natural phenomenon in very unnatural circumstances. This relationship never would have happened if she hadn't been threatened. *Perhaps I should send a proper thank-you note to the man who is trying to kill me.*

When they arrived at her house, he wouldn't allow her to help unload the tons of supplies he'd managed to acquire in the few short hours she'd been at work. After a few feeble objections, she plunked herself down at the kitchen table and watched as he toted in bag after bag of groceries, clothing and equipment.

As he locked the door and set the alarm, she wryly commented, "Looks like you've prepared for a ten-year siege."

"I hate shopping. If I want something, I get it. And I'm not what you'd call selective."

"You're a salesclerk's dream. You just waltz in the door, point and say, 'I'll take ten of those in all colors.'"

"But I only got you one gun." He placed a bag from the sporting goods store on the table. "Go ahead and take a look at it. You might want to pick it up and get accustomed to the heft."

She took out a shiny silver automatic pistol with a black handle. It was purse-sized—bigger than a Black-

Berry but small enough to fit neatly into the zippered pocket on her backpack.

While she got used to her gun, Michael put away the groceries and started the fettuccine parmesan. Though he wasn't wearing a pink apron, the role reversal made her smile. She never would have pegged this man as a cook.

After dinner, he instructed her on the handling of her new pistol. He took it apart and spread out the pieces on the coffee table in front of the sofa, showing her how to insert the ammunition clip. "In like this. Release like this."

"I get it," she said impatiently. Guns had never interested her before, but now she was anxious for hands-on experience.

Michael raised the gun and sited down the barrel. He pivoted and aimed using both hands. His eyes narrowed to a squint. "You need to be relaxed," he drawled. "Centered."

He aimed high with his arm straight and his chin tilted upward. Then his knees bent and he crouched low.

When he illustrated a two-handed marksman's stance with legs spread and knees loose, she realized that she wasn't paying attention to the gun. She was watching him. There was something incredibly sexy about his movements. A lesser man would have looked silly taking aim at invisible enemies, but Michael was as athletic and graceful as a ninja. His wide shoulders tapered to a lean torso and narrow hips. Not an ounce of flab on his body, he was a man built for action. All kinds of action. With very little effort, she imagined him shirtless.

"You want your wrist to be firm," he said. His jeans stretched tight across his thighs as he moved. "Make the gun an extension of your arm."

Shaking herself out of her shameless observation of his masculinity, she rose to her feet. "Let me try."

"A gun isn't a toy," he warned.

"Yes, thank you, Detective." She held out her hand.

"Keep the safety on. Never point it at anyone unless you're prepared to shoot."

She stepped up beside him. "I'm getting the feeling that you're reluctant to hand over the weapon."

"Truth be told, I am."

"Michael, I can take instruction. I won't shoot myself in the foot or anything."

"It's the false expectations that come when you're carrying a lethal weapon." The gravity in his voice caught her attention. "Some people get a sense of being invincible."

"Farthest thing from my mind."

"A gun won't change who you are, Brooke. It takes more than a weapon to make your fears go away."

He didn't have to tell her about being afraid. Not so long ago, terror had been her constant companion. If she could have shaken the cloying grasp of fear by owning a gun, she would have made that purchase long ago. She would have been on the firing range every single day.

"Here's how I see it," she said. "A gun is a tool for protection. I don't expect it to give me courage. That's something I have to find inside myself."

"Something you've already found."

"I have?"

"You're not a coward, Brooke."

In his jade eyes, she saw the gleam of respect. He believed in her, and that belief meant more to her than having him as a bodyguard, more than his caretaking. More than just about anything.

In spite of everything she'd revealed about herself, he didn't think she was pathetic or crazy.

She rested both hands against his chest, aware that the last time she'd done this, it had led to a kiss. An electric surge raced through her veins, arousing every cell in her body. She wanted to be close, to become a part of him. If she kissed him now, there would be no stopping.

"I'm not afraid," she whispered.

Never in her life had she made love to a man she'd known for only a few days. She'd always been a good girl, playing it safe.

"It's up to you," he said.

She hesitated. Now might not be the best time. She'd almost died this morning—it had been a long day, to put it mildly. She pulled her hands away. "Maybe tomorrow."

"Isn't that what Scarlett O'Hara always said?"

"Tomorrow is another day," she quoted. "A wise woman, that Scarlett."

She turned and went upstairs. Before she could change her mind, she got into pajamas and dove between the sheets. Exhaustion caught up with her almost instantly, and she was asleep in seconds.

But she didn't make it through the whole night. She woke with a start a few minutes past one. She'd been dreaming of Michael, of what it would be like to feel his body pressed against hers.

She turned on the bedside lamp.

She wasn't Scarlett O'Hara. She was a practical woman who knew what she wanted and went for it. *Forget about tomorrow. Another day is a day too long.*

As soon as she stepped outside her bedroom door, she saw him, half-naked, pistol in hand.

"What's wrong?" he asked.

"Absolutely nothing."

She crossed to him, sliding her arms around his neck, pulling him toward her. And then she kissed him for all she was worth.

Chapter Fourteen

Brooke's sensual dream became reality. Michael kissed her back with a passionate heat that melted any lingering thought of resistance. They had held back long enough. It was time for this kiss, this fire. He pulled her close. Her breasts crushed against his chest.

Her senses reeled as she clung to him, greedy for more. "My bed," she said.

Almost before she was aware of what was happening, they were there. The glow from her bedside lamp reminded her that she wasn't dreaming. Michael was here. In her bedroom. Here in this solitary cell where she came to meditate and find peace. The room filled with an unfamiliar frenzy of excitement.

His hand slid under her pajama top. He cupped her breast, teased the nipple. Was he still holding his pistol? She gasped out one word. "Gun?"

"On the bedside table." He paused looking down at her. "You know, Brooke, I don't take aim unless I intend to shoot. Is this what you want?"

She gazed into his deep-set jade eyes. Was this what she wanted? She reached for him, caressing the sandpaper stubble on his firm jaw. "Yes, Michael."

As they stared at each other, memorizing the moment, he unbuttoned her red flannel pajamas, patterned with snowflakes. Not exactly the most seductive nightwear in the world. But he didn't seem to care as he pushed the fabric aside and leaned down to nuzzle her breasts.

Excitement burned inside her. She couldn't stay still. Her back arched, thrusting toward him. She wanted his mouth on hers again.

His kiss was hard and demanding. His fingers tangled in her hair. Every move he made gave her pleasure in a new way. Another stroke. Another caress. Her pajama top was off. Her naked flesh met his. His muscular chest and lean torso were perfect, exactly what she wanted.

With a few more skillful maneuvers, the rest of their clothing was shed. His thigh stretched across her, pinning her to the bed. "I need to go back to my room. Just for a minute," he whispered in her ear.

"Why?" She didn't want to be apart from him. Not even for a minute.

"Protection."

She yanked open the drawer of her bedside table. "I have condoms."

A slow, sultry, Southern grin spread across his face. "Surprise, surprise."

She grinned back at him. "I never gave up hope."

Even in her wildest dreams, she never imagined that making love would feel so exactly right. With every touch, he aroused another wave of quivering sensation. He knew when to kiss, when to pull back and when to thrust hard. Her climax was bigger and better than anything she'd ever experienced before.

Afterward, she lay beside him, safe in his arms, daring to sleep deeply without fear of nightmares.

THE NEXT morning, Brooke tried to get up and get ready for work as usual. But there was nothing ordinary about this day. Because Michael was with her. Michael Shaw, her lover.

She'd never expected her life to turn out this way. During her divorce, she'd decided that she didn't want anything more to do with men and might as well join a nunnery or become a hermit, free from any entanglement. Instead, she'd stumbled into a relationship with a Southern gentleman who really knew how to treat a woman.

He had woken her with a gentle kiss that quickly became passionate. He was inside her again and driving her crazy before she was even fully awake. She felt like the luckiest woman alive.

Afterward, she slipped on her robe went downstairs to start the coffee for him. After yesterday, she didn't have much taste for fresh-brewed. Instead, she'd have herbal tea—no sugar. Mug in hand, she went to the sliding glass doors that opened onto the deck. Puffy snowflakes drifted down from gray skies. For the first time since Michael had arrived, it was snowing.

Snowfall was always welcome at a ski resort, especially around Christmastime, but she was so happy she'd expected bright sunshine to greet her. The gloomy weather served as a reminder that all was not well.

Michael came up behind her and rested a hand on her shoulder. "Looks cold."

"But you bought a ton of new winter clothing yesterday. You'll be toasty."

"Let's stay here today. Just you and me. We've got plenty of food, and I think we can come up with enough activities to keep ourselves occupied."

"I'd like that." She leaned back against him. "But I do need to keep my job."

And my life on track. Michael wouldn't be staying here forever. When the threat to her safety was over, he'd be headed back to his life as a cop in Birmingham.

"The weather could get worse," he said. "You could take a snow day."

"If everybody in Aspen took off work when it snowed, the town would have to close down."

In a few weeks, it would be Christmas, and he'd want to be surrounded by his family. She'd be alone, again. Before she sank too deeply into the Christmas blues, she reminded herself that being alone was far preferable to being with her ex-husband.

And she had this moment in time, these hours she could spend with Michael. The lazy snowflakes began to pile up on the branches of the pine trees outside the window.

"I'm going to work," she said. "And I'm taking the gun."

He leaned down to nibble at the lobe of her ear. "First, you need a shower."

Moments ago, she'd been thoroughly satisfied. But his kiss started her engine going again. "A shower sounds good. You could join me."

"You're reading my mind."

They raced up the stairs to the bathroom. Under the hot, steaming water, they soaped each other's bodies, taking their time, enjoying the sensations. She couldn't keep her hands off him—especially his tight butt. He was gorgeous. Maybe she really was the luckiest woman alive.

"I can't believe this is happening," she said.

"It was inevitable." He turned around and faced her. "You're a damn desirable woman. I was attracted to you the first minute I saw you in the boutique."

"A lot has happened since then."

"Nothing that changes my first impression."

"Now you're just being gallant." She rubbed the soap on his chest, working up a lather. "I haven't exactly been charming."

"Sure, you have."

"Michael, when you first came to the house, I threatened you with a kitchen knife."

"An understandable error."

"Then I burst into tears," she said. "I'm amazed that you didn't run for the hills. Then I made it worse by blabbing all my horrible, miserable, shameful life secrets."

"And I thank you for sharing that intimate part of yourself." His hands glided down her body. "Honesty is a very attractive trait."

"Obviously, you're just saying that because you want a little nookie. It's not necessary to bribe me with compliments, Michael."

"I'm telling the truth."

"Really? I can't wait to hear how you're going to put a positive spin on yesterday morning's puke fest."

"Not entirely adorable," he drawled. "And I generally don't enjoy the role of nursemaid. But I certainly did like combing your hair and massaging your feet. I'd do it again in a heartbeat."

He seemed to have an answer for everything. *All the right answers.* She wanted him again—and he was happy to oblige.

BACK IN Birmingham, snow was as rare as a three-legged rooster. Even so, Michael preferred being the one behind the steering wheel, which probably proved Brooke's often-repeated accusation that he was a control freak. Ironic. He didn't feel like he was in control of anything—definitely not the beautiful, blue-eyed lady who sat in the passenger seat, checking her cell phone. Every time he glanced in her direction, his libido ran amok. Common sense flew out the window. He wanted to make love to her every hour of every day for the foreseeable future.

As he drove along the curving canyon road toward Aspen with the light snow falling in a ragged curtain, his grip on the steering wheel tensed. This kind of rampant lust wasn't the way he did things. He planned. He organized. He took one logical step after another and didn't allow his emotions to get the best of him.

"Did I mention," she asked, "that I had a phone call from Tammy Gallegos?"

"You did." For a moment, his sexual urges took second place to the indelible mental checklist that was always focused on the serial killings. Tammy had already left the country. She was in a faraway land, and Michael didn't have to worry about what might happen to her.

"I have a message here from a lawyer who works for Sally's parents. He's instructing me to ship all her belongings to a Colorado Springs address and says he'll reimburse my expenses."

"But her parents haven't called?"

When Brooke shook her head, the tassel on the top of her knitted cap bounced from side to side. "Doesn't that seem cold to you? I never met Sally's parents, but it seems like they'd want to talk to me. I was her roommate."

"People handle tragedy in all kinds of ways, especially when it comes to homicide. Maybe they just want to be left alone."

Her nose wrinkled in a frown that he found adorable. He wanted to park right now in the middle of the road and kiss her silly. Making love in a Hummer would be fine with him.

"Sally never talked about her parents," she said. "Maybe they were estranged. Like her husband."

"Seems that your roommate didn't do well with long-term relationships, not even with her kinfolk." The detective part of his brain registered the fact that Sally's parents were on the other side of the globe when she was murdered and couldn't possibly be considered as suspects. "She flitted from one place to another. From one boyfriend to another."

"But they'll probably have a service. I should go, shouldn't I?"

"If you're not invited, you aren't obliged to attend."

That unhappy task would be left to the CBI detectives. Funerals and the like were always a good place to observe potential suspects.

"Maybe," Brooke said, "I should put together some kind of memorial here. In Aspen."

A memorial for Sally would be a gathering place for all the people who might have wanted her dead—the boyfriends she'd dumped and the girlfriends who'd had their men stolen—but he didn't want Brooke to be standing in the middle of that crowd.

When it came right down to it, he didn't even want her working at the boutique. He wanted to surround her with ten-inch-thick walls of bulletproof glass to protect her like the precious treasure she was. Maybe he should just sling her over his shoulder and carry her off to Birmingham where he could be certain that she was well-guarded.

He dared to sneak a peek in her direction. Her insulated jacket betrayed very little of her shape, but he had memorized her curves. The fullness of her hips. The graceful arch of her back. Her round, perfect breasts.

"Michael?"

Unwillingly, he pulled back from his fantasizing. "Huh?"

"I'd like to get my car from the hotel today."

"There's no need. We're going to be together 24-7, and I'll do the driving."

"It's still handy to have two vehicles at the house."

He couldn't imagine why, unless they were both driving at the same time, which meant they'd be separated, which didn't fit with his plans. "I'm going to have to say no."

"Control freak," she muttered. "If I really want my car, I can get it myself and—"

"Enough," he relented. "We'll get your car."

"Thank you," she said sweetly.

Her sly little grin told him that she was patently aware that she'd won the battle for control. "But don't think you've got me flummoxed."

"Flummoxed? There's a word you don't hear every day."

"My Uncle Elmo had a billy goat that he said got flummoxed when he became infatuated with one of the barn cats. Poor old billy bleated, ran around in circles and didn't know his head from his tail."

"I can't see that happening to you," she said. "Are you warm enough?"

"Blazing hot."

"I like your new winter gear."

On his shopping trip the day before, he'd purchased a waterproof, insulated skiing jacket in chocolate brown that was surprisingly light. The attached hood would come in handy in the snow today. On his feet, he wore hiking boots with insulation inserts. "The best part is the silk thermal underwear."

"Why aren't you wearing the pants that go with the jacket?"

"A man's gotta draw the line somewhere." She laughed. "I'd feel like a fraud if I put on the whole costume."

"You should try skiing while you're here. You're not afraid of a few slips and falls, are you?"

He'd been watching the snowboarders as they came down the slopes, and it didn't look all that different from skateboarding—except for the incline. "I don't mind sliding down the mountain on my rump while I get the hang of it. The problem is that I can't be a bodyguard and snowboarder at the same time."

"Really? Do you think Jackson is going to come schussing down the slope, grab me and zoom away?"

"He might try to get you alone." The Hummer rounded the final curve and came out of the forest. In the light snowfall, Aspen looked like an ideal version of Christmas. "So far, his attempts on your life have been designed to look like suicide. But there are a lot of ways he could arrange for you to have a fatal accident."

She shuddered. "I'm glad I have a gun in my backpack."

Michael didn't think a gun was going to be much good against a schemer like Jackson Warren. But he kept his mouth shut.

Chapter Fifteen

After he parked at the hotel lot, Michael walked Brooke to work where a couple of customers were already browsing. Hannah was working on a spectacular Christmas window display. He headed toward the Pitkin County Courthouse for another talk with McGraw. As luck would have it, he caught the deputy coming out the front door.

Without wasting any time, McGraw rumbled, "I've got bad news. And more bad news. Which do you want to hear first?"

"You want to talk here?"

"Why not?"

Michael peered out from his hood at the falling snow. It seemed that people in Aspen didn't run for cover unless they got hit with a blizzard. "Start with the bad."

"Our forensic lab found ground-up drugs in your sugar container. Pain medications. They gave me the complete chemical breakdown."

Michael didn't understand—drugs in the sugar seemed to prove his theory. "Tell me why this is bad news."

"It's an exact match for prescription drugs that turned up in our inventory of the house. The pain meds belonged to Sally. They were readily available in the house."

Which meant that if Brooke had been suicidal, she could have doctored the sugar herself. This guy was good, that's for sure. "That sure doesn't help my case against Jackson Warren."

"Nope." McGraw puffed out his lips below his thick mustache. "I like you, Michael. I think you're a good cop and a loyal friend who's having a hard time getting over the murder of your buddy back in Atlanta. That's why I'm going to sit on this information and not turn it over to the CBI or the FBI or any other kind of bureau. If those boys start looking at Brooke as a suicide risk, they might think she's dangerous in other ways."

"I appreciate that you're keeping this to yourself." He didn't want the wrong kind of attention focused on Brooke. "What's the other bad news?"

"We got the autopsy results. That little needle mark found by our coroner was real important. Sally was shot up with a powerful sedative. Not enough to kill her but enough to render her unconscious. Those bumps and bruises on her were from before she died."

"She taught snowboarding," Michael said. "If she took a fall, she'd likely get banged up."

"Not like this. She had bruises on her face and head. The autopsy suggests that she was dragged some distance. And was unconscious when she got strung up."

"So, this case is definitely homicide." Not a surprise. Michael had drawn that conclusion long ago.

McGraw's mustache twitched. "You understand why this is bad news."

"Not exactly."

"Sally wasn't a big woman. A man would have picked her up and carried her instead of dragging her unconscious body across the floor."

Michael winced. "A woman might have dragged her."

"That's the theory." McGraw brushed the accumulating snow off his jacket. "For what it's worth, I don't believe Brooke is a killer."

But she was, according to the other investigators, a very viable suspect.

AT THE boutique, Brooke rang up matching cashmere scarves for a tall, willowy supermodel from Argentina and her equally gorgeous companion. It was hard to keep from staring at those high cheekbones, full lips and dramatic eyes.

When the couple left, she turned to Hannah. "Wow."

"In all the years I've been in Aspen, I still get starstruck when the celebrities arrive for winter skiing. You handled her well," Hannah said.

"She was nice," Brooke said. "In addition to being just about the most perfect creature I've ever seen. Wow."

"Brace yourself, honey. By Christmas, you'll have seen Academy Award winners, rock stars and royalty. I once sold a ski cap to Princess Di. The whole time she was in the shop, I wanted to curtsy."

Hannah chuckled as she reached up to smooth her short, gray hair. As usual, she wore all black with her silver concha belt. Her accessory for the day was a pair of large Christmas tree earrings. "Speaking of gorgeous creatures, how are things going with your bodyguard?"

"Michael's fine."

"That's not what I'm asking, honey."

Brooke had never been the type to blab about her personal life, possibly because there hadn't been much to blab about. But she couldn't resist today. "Michael's wonderful. We're having a…" What were they having? Not a relationship, because that implied something long term. Calling their time together an affair sounded cheap. "We're friends."

"Bosom buddies?"

Brooke felt herself begin to blush. "Bosoms might be involved."

"Good for you. I was beginning to worry about why an attractive, healthy young woman like you never dated."

Because I was too scared to open my eyes. The realization struck like a thunderbolt. After all the trauma of the past few years, she'd been purposely blind. Being with Michael helped her conquer her fears. All her fears. As well as that nagging doubt that she would ever want to make love again.

"Brooke? Are you all right?"

"Never better," she said honestly.

Hannah stuck her hands on her hips. "Don't you let that handsome cop break your heart when he leaves town."

"Don't worry."

She'd had plenty of experience in keeping her heart guarded and knew better than to expect anything more from Michael than a whirlwind romance—a precious gift. Of course, it would hurt when he left. But now she had the strength to heal.

A commotion outside the shop drew both women to the front window. The snowfall had dwindled to occasional flurries, and the sun tried to break through the heavy, gray clouds. In contrast, the town square was a kaleidoscope of color, mainly people dressed in red and green. Saturdays during ski season were usually busy, but this was extraordinary.

Brooke spotted a camera crew. "What's going on?"

"Snowboard Santas." Hannah leaned forward to see. "A

couple of years back, when all these kids with snowboards started showing up, I thought they'd be nothing more than troublemakers who got in the way of the real skiers. But I've changed my mind. I admire their gumption."

"Why are they marching around?"

"Snowboard Santas start with a ragtag parade. Then they auction off two hours of snowboarding with one of the famous snowboarders—the X Games superstars—or one of the instructors. The money they raise goes to Children's Hospital in Denver."

Tyler Hennessey was sure to be on the short list of super snowboarders. Brooke shrank back from the window, not wanting another encounter with that local celeb.

Four guys with reindeer horns carried a throne with the official Snowboard Santa—a young man with long brown hair and a scraggly beard. His Santa cap was pulled down over his ears.

"That kid almost won the Olympics," Hannah said. "He's a cutie, isn't he? Do you mind if I step outside to get a better view?"

"That depends. Are you planning to bid on Santa?"

"I might."

"Then don't let me stand in your way."

Hannah rushed to the back of the shop to grab her jacket and then went outside. Brooke stayed at the window, enjoying the party atmosphere of the crowd. Sally would have loved this moment; she probably would have been auctioned off as an expert snowboarder. All the guys she'd dated would have bid higher and higher for the favors of the popular party girl.

Then she probably would have brought a crowd of Santas back to the house for a party that would have kept

Brooke up all night. In a strange way, she missed the chaos and noise that always accompanied her roommate. A tear slid down her cheek, and she quickly wiped it away. Sally would have laughed to find her crying.

Determinedly, Brooke focused on the antics of the snowboarders. Some dressed like elves. Several wore red Santa caps and chanted, "Ho, ho, ho." At the edge of the crowd, she noticed a man, dressed in a black parka with the hood pulled up. He'd turned away from the crowd and seemed to be staring at the shop. Staring at her. He took a step in her direction.

He was jostled and drawn into a clumsy polka. His hood fell back. He looked familiar—her blood froze in her veins before she even realized why.

He pulled up his hood and turned away. Was it him? Was it Jackson Warren? His face seemed too narrow. There were gaunt hollows under his cheekbones as if he'd been ill.

Peering hard, she tried to catch another glimpse. With all the dancing and parading, she couldn't see, didn't know for sure.

This morning on the drive into town, Michael said that Jackson might try to get her alone. The shop was empty. There was no one here to protect her.

Why was she wasting time standing here like a statue? If she'd actually seen Jackson in the town square, she'd better be ready for him. Forcing her legs to move, she went to the back of the shop and found her backpack.

Her fingers fumbled with the zipper. Was she over-reacting? Seeing things that weren't there? She'd gotten a good look at the guy, but she couldn't be sure it was him, couldn't really identify him from a computer photo.

She lifted the gun from her pack. Better to be safe and look like a fool than to be sorry that she hadn't been prepared.

Following Michael's instructions, she shoved an ammunition clip into the automatic pistol and readied it to shoot. Last night, Michael had shown her several positions. Always taking aim. Always holding the gun at the ready, prepared to shoot. Could she? Could she pull the trigger?

Her hand trembled. Adrenaline poured through her system. Her heart pounded against her rib cage.

She was afraid. Of course she was afraid. But this was different than before. She had a clear, logical reason for being frightened. A serial killer was threatening her. Fear was the appropriate response—the only response.

She peeked around the wall separating the crowded storeroom at the back of the shop from the front display area. No one had entered. If they had, she would have heard the bell above the door jingle.

Oh, Michael, where are you?

He'd warned her that Jackson might try to grab her and carry her off to arrange an accidental death. There were so many ways to die in the mountains. Falling from a cliff. Being buried in snow. Freezing and going into hypothermia. A rock slide. An avalanche.

She would never allow him to take her prisoner. Fearful? Yes. But she would fight.

Setting down the gun, she dug into her backpack and found her cell phone. She punched in the number for Michael's cell. He answered on the second ring. "What's up?"

"Jackson Warren," she whispered. "I saw him."

"Where are you?"

"In the boutique. There's a lot of craziness going on outside." She tried to keep her voice level and controlled. "What should I do?"

"Stay put. I'll be there in less than ten minutes."

The phone went dead in her hand, and she imagined Michael running toward her.

She checked the back door to the shop, making sure it was locked and so no one could come inside from that direction. Holding her gun and moving on silent feet, she crept into the front of the shop and ducked behind the counter. Not much of a hiding place, but she felt safer in here than mingling with the noisy crowd outside the door. If he grabbed her amid that chaos, nobody would notice. They'd assume her screams were part of the fun. But she'd never been more serious in her life.

Hardly daring to breathe, she waited. *Please, Michael. Hurry.*

Then she heard the jingle of the bell above the door. Someone had entered the shop.

Chapter Sixteen

Brooke knew it wasn't Michael who had entered the boutique; he would have announced himself. It might be a customer, an innocent shopper looking for a new pair of sunglasses. She listened for the sound of footsteps on the hardwood floor. Noise from the crowd filtered inside. Otherwise, it was quiet. She didn't hear the rattle of hangers or the whisper of fabrics.

She eased her way to a crouch and peeked over the counter. No one was there. But she'd heard the bell. Someone had opened the door.

With the gun braced in both hands, she stood. Fear trembled through her. He was close. She knew the killer was close at hand.

"Hello?" Her voice quavered. "Is anybody here?"

She glimpsed movement and turned, raising the gun and sighting down the barrel the way Michael showed her. A filmy scarf tied around the throat of a mannequin fluttered in response to her motion.

The shop wasn't that big. They didn't have a dressing room. There was no place he could hide.

But she'd heard the bell.

And she'd seen him, standing outside the shop and

staring at her. A face at the window. Like the face she'd seen outside the sliding glass door at her house. Not a delusion.

Michael burst through the door. The tension that gripped her dissipated in a whoosh of relief. Michael's energy filled the room as he made quick work of searching.

Trembling, she stood at the counter. "I didn't imagine him. I saw him."

"I know."

He wrapped his arms around her. His gloved hand stroked her back. The front of his jacket was damp and cold against her cheek. When she looked up at him, she saw his usually tidy hair standing up in wet spikes.

"He was standing outside," she said, "staring at me."

"What was he wearing?"

"A jacket with a hood. Black or maybe a really dark blue. And I think he had on jeans." She tried to give a useful description. "His face was skinnier than in the photograph. Kind of sunken. Like he's been sick."

"I hope so." He kissed her forehead.

"There really wasn't anything unusual about him. Average height. Bundled up in winter clothes. He looks like half the men in town."

His glove traced the line of her chin. "It would have been nice if he'd been draped in hot pink, but he's accustomed to blending in. Unless he wants to stand out, he won't."

Having him with her bolstered her courage. Though her heart was still racing, she felt stronger. "It helped for me to be armed. Fortunately, I didn't accidentally shoot a supermodel or a movie star."

"Very fortunate." Though he smiled, worry lines creased his forehead. "He's out there, Brooke. I need to go after him."

"No way are you leaving me here by myself."

"I'll take you to the courthouse. McGraw can protect you."

She'd spent too much of her life being intimidated, cowering in a corner like a frightened mouse. She hadn't transformed into a lioness—not yet, anyway—but she didn't want to hide. "I'm the one who saw him. I'll recognize his clothes if I see him again."

"Makes sense," he admitted. "Stick close to me. Under no circumstances are we to be separated."

"Got it."

Hannah came through the door and saw the guns. Though Brooke hadn't told her the whole story, Hannah knew that Michael was acting as a bodyguard. Her brows pulled into a frown. "What can I do?"

"I have to leave," Brooke said as she went to the rear of the shop for her backpack. She slipped into her jacket and her Peruvian knitted cap. "I'll be back."

"Take care," Hannah said. "Both of you."

OUTSIDE, MICHAEL analyzed their situation from a tactical standpoint. The crowd was both a plus and a minus. If Jackson attempted to harm Brooke, there were enough people in the way to make it difficult for him to escape. But the mob scene made it hard to search for one individual dressed in winter clothing like everybody else.

They needed a vantage point where Brooke could survey the scene and, hopefully, make an identification. He maneuvered her toward the steps leading to the Silver Queen gondola. Skiers who weren't involved in the Snowboard Santa melee were still boarding the small six-person gondolas and being whisked up the mountain.

To make matters worse, the snowfall was picking up

again. Michael wanted to pull up the hood on his jacket but didn't dare obscure his peripheral vision.

"This would be a lot easier in the South," he said. "With all these hoods, it's hard to see anybody's face."

"And a lot of these people are wearing dark jackets and jeans. Like you."

The auctioneer, obviously a professional from his fast-talking patter, started taking bids. Michael asked, "What are they selling?"

"Time with a superstar snowboarder," she said. "The money goes to charity."

"Good to know that this craziness has a purpose. These people aren't all lunatics."

But one of them might be a killer.

In the interest of crowd safety, he kept his gun holstered on his belt. Brooke's weapon was tucked away in her backpack. He didn't think they looked like a lethal threat—they were just another couple, enjoying the auction.

A blond woman approached Brooke. Her lower lip quivered. "I can't believe you're wearing Sally's jacket."

Brooke was startled. "It's actually mine," she finally said. "I didn't even know Sally had borrowed it."

"Oh, right. She did that a lot, didn't she? She always—"

"I can't talk right now," Brooke said. "I'm sorry."

Michael pulled her away. It wouldn't be too difficult to keep track of her in the crowd. Her multicolored, wool hat with the tassel on top made her stand out.

"I'm going to have to get rid of this jacket," she muttered. "I can't walk around in clothes Sally used to wear."

"Forget about your wardrobe. We have bigger concerns." He turned her toward the auction. "Do you see him?"

"It's hard to tell."

A cheer went through the crowd as one of the Snow-board Santas was auctioned off for four hundred and thirty dollars.

"If Jackson Warren is still out here," Michael said, "he's using the crowd for cover. Look into the clusters of people."

Someone else came toward them. Michael recognized Peter Thorne, the ski patrol guy they'd met outside the hotel. Just like their last encounter, Peter smelled like beer.

"Hey, Brooke." His dark eyes were angry. "When I first looked over here and saw you, I thought you were Sally. You really look alike. I miss her."

Brooke responded, "Sorry, Peter."

"You know what? I got fired."

"Sorry," she repeated.

"Maybe I could stop by your place sometime. You know, to talk about Sally or something."

Michael had to put an end to this conversation. He needed Brooke to focus on the crowd. "She's with me."

"Yeah? Well, that never stopped Sally. She was with everybody. Know what I mean?"

Another man in a ski patrol parka turned toward them. "Don't talk about her that way."

"Who's going to stop me? You?"

"There's a reason you got fired, Peter. You need to lay off the booze."

A huge, heavyset man—big as a mountain—came up behind Peter. "What's up? This dude giving you trouble, Pete?"

Michael could see what was about to happen next. Combined with the party atmosphere and the snow, he was looking at impending chaos. And he wanted to get Brooke away from here.

As he turned to pull her away, Peter grabbed his arm. "Where are you going? I'm still talking."

Michael shook off his grasp. It would have been simple to take Peter down, but he didn't want to start a riot. Calmly, he said, "We have to go."

Peter took a clumsy swing at him, and Michael easily blocked the blow. The mountain-sized guy lunged forward. Three men in ski patrol jackets got involved. In spite of the confusion of pushing, yelling and drunken punching, Michael extricated himself quickly.

But not quickly enough.

When he looked around, Brooke was gone.

A MUSCULAR arm clamped around her waist, lifting her off her feet. Brooke couldn't see the man who grabbed her. Everything happened too fast.

She tried to wrench free. He tightened his grip, squeezing her midsection hard. Panic crashed through her brain as he dragged her into the crowd near the gondola. Why wasn't anyone helping her? She tried to gasp out a plea but he laughed, pretending that he was teasing her and playing a game so no one would look twice.

He moved fast, rushing through the crowd. She couldn't stop him. In his grip, she was a rag doll, yanked along at his will.

Her only coherent thought was to hang on to her backpack. If she had her gun, she wasn't helpless. She tried to unzip the pocket as he carried her.

They cut through the line of people waiting for gondolas. He shoved her into a car and she sprawled on the rubberized floor mats. He closed the door and locked it. The gondola took off with a swoop.

She was trapped, locked in a small compartment with

floor-to-ceiling windows, suspended above the slopes. Trapped with a killer.

Still on the floor, she reached into her backpack, grabbed her gun and pointed it at her kidnapper. "Tyler?"

"Whoa!" Tyler Hennessey backed up against the glass, his hands raised. "Don't shoot."

Without lowering the gun, she hauled herself up on one of the benches. The fact that she'd been abducted by Tyler explained a lot. The lift operators knew him and allowed him to cut to the head of the line. No one had attempted to help her because Tyler Hennessey was a local celebrity—people assumed she wanted to be with him.

Wrong assumption! She despised this pushy, self-important jerk. "I ought to blow off your kneecap."

"Feisty." He dared to grin at her. "Come on, Brooke. I just wanted to get you alone so we could talk."

"So you kidnapped me? Threw me in a gondola?" Her finger twitched on the trigger. "Did you ever hear of a phone?"

"Dude." He shook his head. His streaky blond hair fell across his forehead. "I was pretty sure you'd hang up on me."

She gestured with the gun. "Sit on that bench, put your hands on your head and don't move. If I have the tiniest hint that you're threatening me, I will shoot. Got it, *dude?*"

He plunked down on the seat while she pulled out her cell phone and called Michael. As soon as he answered, she said, "I'm all right. Tyler Hennessey grabbed me and dragged me into a gondola."

"Tell me you're not hurt." The concern in his voice touched her. "You're not injured in any way."

"I'm fine. Tyler wanted to talk."

"Tyler." He snarled the word. "If there's one bruise on

your body or one hair out of place on your head, you can tell that snowboarding chump that he's a dead man."

"Nice attitude for a cop. Aren't you supposed to support the legal system? Advise me to press assault charges or something?" she said, keeping an eye on Tyler, who was looking more concerned by the minute.

"Are you really okay?" His voice lowered to an intimate level. "Tell me, Brooke."

"I'm fine, Michael. I promise. I'll see you when I get down."

With a snap, she disconnected the call. Right now, she was feeling pretty good. No fear. Tyler, on the other hand, looked sheepish and embarrassed, aware that he had made a big mistake.

"First," she said, "I want an apology. Keep in mind that my name isn't 'dude.'"

"I'm sorry."

She nodded acceptance. "You can put your hands down. Now tell me what's so important that you'd risk arrest to talk to me."

"I wanted you to know how I felt about Sally. I really liked her a lot. The way she'd laugh and tease. That girl could drink anybody under the table."

A lovely quality in a mate. What man wouldn't be captivated by excessive alcohol consumption? "Uh-huh."

"When she dumped me, it hurt real bad."

Outside the window of the gondola, the snow fell more steadily. Though it was noontime and the sun should have been shining, the towering pines on either side of the gondola car faded into gray shadows.

She worried that Tyler might be about to confess to murder. She might be trapped in a gondola with a person capable of homicide. Still, somehow, she wasn't afraid—

she was in control. "Did you want to hurt her back? Show her how it felt?"

"I was plenty mad," he said. "But I could never hurt Sally. I loved her."

Brooke saw genuine pain in his eyes. Gone was his cocky, king-of-the-mountain attitude.

"Why did Sally break up with you?" she asked.

"Same old story. Another dude. And this guy wasn't even a snowboarder. He looked like a businessman or something."

Her suspicions were piqued. Choosing a boring businessman over Tyler the Superstar didn't sound like something Sally would have done. "What was his name?"

"Don't know. He wasn't local."

"Was he wealthy?"

Tyler shrugged. "What difference does that make? I mean, hey, if she was looking for bucks, I'm flush. I just signed another fat endorsement deal."

And Sally had recently received an influx of cash, enough that she intended to start paying her husband back. "Did you ever loan money to Sally?"

"I would have, but she never asked."

Her extra money had come from somewhere else. Someone else. The new boyfriend? "Did you ever meet him?"

"Not like a real introduction or anything. I saw them together on the street, and I yelled to her. She pushed him out of the way and came at me like a bobcat. Told me to get lost. She was busy."

"What did you say?"

"I told her I was a one-woman man, and I didn't want her hanging out with some other guy. And she said that maybe she'd rather be with a guy who knew how to treat a lady, a guy who knew the right words to say."

Like a con man who could sweet-talk his way into just about anything. Brooke dug into her backpack and took out the computer photo of Jackson Warren. She held it up.

"That's him," Tyler said. "That's the dude."

Chapter Seventeen

When Michael saw Brooke emerge from the gondola with Tyler, his temper roared like the start to the Indy 500. He was in no mood for Tyler Hennessey, not after what he'd been through.

A half an hour ago, he'd turned around and she was gone. His heart had stopped. He'd thought she'd fallen victim to Jackson Warren's terrible vendetta. And he'd been destroyed. Couldn't react. Couldn't think.

To be sure, there had been other times in his life when he hadn't been sure of his strategy. But his confusion in that moment had been overwhelming. Search? Run? Pull his pistol and arrest every one of those dancing Santas and reindeer? He hadn't known what to do. And he wasn't used to that.

Along with the bone-chilling regret that came from failing in his mission to guard her, he suffered a deeper sense of loss, as if a vital piece of his life had been shredded. Until that moment, he didn't comprehend what she was to him. He didn't want to be separated from her. Not for a moment. Not ever.

She and Tyler stopped in front of him, and she nudged the arrogant snowboarder's arm.

Tyler gave a nod and said, "I'm sorry."

Michael couldn't force a civil reply through his lips, not now while his fingers were itching to rip that foolish grin off Tyler's face.

Brooke seemed to comprehend the depth and range of his barely restrained fury because she took Michael's arm and led him back toward the boutique.

"I have information," she said. "Wait until you hear this."

He came to an abrupt halt in the middle of the square. The Snowboard Santa auction was over, and the town had gone back to a normal level of activity. The snow kept falling. The wind kept blowing. If he hadn't been so angry, he would have been freezing cold. "I can't let him off with nothing more than a half-baked apology."

"What do you want to do?"

"Firing squad."

"You're going to forget all about being mad when you hear this."

"Tell."

"Remember how we suspected Tyler because he got dumped when Sally got involved with another man? Part of that is true. There was a new boyfriend, and Tyler saw him. He wasn't a local. Not a skier. And Sally said her new guy knew exactly the right thing to say at the right time. He was a smooth talker."

"Get to the point."

"I showed him the picture, and Tyler made the identification. Sally's new boyfriend was Stonewall Jackson Warren."

Jackson and Sally? Michael hadn't seen this coming.

"Here's what I think happened," Brooke continued. "Jackson was snooping around and met Sally by accident. He said that he was infatuated with her, which Sally would have readily believed because everybody was infatuated with her. But when she figured out what he was *really* after, he had to kill her."

Michael wasn't surprised that she'd come up with a scenario that made her roommate look innocent. Brooke wanted to believe the best of other people—even her annoying roommate. He suspected the truth would betray a much darker side to Sally Klinger.

From what her husband said, Sally was a clever salesperson, not above pulling scams of her own. She and Jackson had that in common. "Jackson could have recruited Sally to work with him. He might have paid her to help him."

"That doesn't make sense." She shook her head. "If they were dating, Sally would have welcomed him into the house. She hardly ever kept the doors locked."

"Arranging your murder to look like suicide would have been complicated. He needed to bring in the rope. To access your computer journal. To make sure Sally wouldn't be there as a witness."

"Are you saying that he paid Sally to help him murder me?"

"That's exactly what I'm saying." He took her arm and guided her toward the boutique. "You need to take the rest of the day off so I can get you to safety."

"You're wrong about Sally. She had a wild streak, but she wasn't a murderer."

"You didn't know her, Brooke. You lived in the same house, but you never talked to each other."

"We talked," she said defensively. "Sally wouldn't have been part of a plot to kill me."

"You didn't know her parents spent the winter in New Zealand. You didn't know she was married. And you didn't keep track of her boyfriends."

"But murder?"

"On some level, you ought to be relieved. Sally's murder wasn't your fault. She brought this on herself when she conspired with a killer."

She dug in her heels and came to a halt outside the boutique. "I don't want to leave Hannah in the lurch for the rest of today. It's a Saturday in ski season."

"Don't even think about arguing with me. You're in immediate danger. We know Jackson is in town, and he's getting desperate, which is why he risked exposure. I wouldn't put it past him to make a direct assault."

"What kind of assault?"

He could tell she was irritated from the glint in her eyes and the tension around her mouth, but her anger was nothing compared to the fury building inside him. "He wants you dead. That could mean a sniper bullet through the glass in the boutique window. A garrote. A switch-blade. An explosion."

"You're exaggerating." But her voice was shaky. "A bomb?"

In war zones, Michael had firsthand experience with suicide bombers. He'd seen the terrible devastation. "He made Grant's murder look like an execution. Jackson might try just about anything, and we're a couple of fools to be standing here, allowing him a clear shot. We're going to the hotel. You can call Hannah from there."

BROOKE STORMED into the hotel suite. The tasteful, perfectly cleaned space did nothing to smooth her ruffled feathers. She wheeled around to confront Michael.

"You're wasting a ton of money holding this room. We haven't slept here since the first night."

"It gives me peace of mind." Looking anything but

peaceful, he went to the windows and whipped the curtains closed. His Southern gentleman veneer had begun to show cracks. "This is a safe place for us to stay."

"Why?" She'd had enough of his cranky, controlling attitude. Not that she intended to do anything risky. "You went to extreme lengths to turn my house into a fortress. I want to go there. After I pick up my car from the parking garage."

"I need to make a couple of phone calls," he said. "Then we'll decide what to do next."

"Don't even think that you'll get me to change my mind."

He was already on his cell phone, ignoring her. Now that the investigation seemed to be on the fast track, he had no more use for her. She was yesterday's victim.

Brooke took off her jacket and her cap, draping them on the chair. Running her fingers through her curls probably wouldn't cure a bad case of hat hair, but she didn't care. Her appearance didn't matter. Not anymore. Her time with Michael was running out, like the inevitable sands through the hourglass.

She flung herself onto the long sectional sofa and stared into the unlit fireplace. She imagined that she was seeing the dead ashes of their relationship. Their lovemaking last night burned with wild abandon. Now it was doused.

As soon as Michael got McGraw and his men on the lookout, Jackson Warren would be taken into custody. She'd be safe. And Michael would head back to Birmingham where he belonged.

At the very least, he ought to thank her. She'd made the connection between Sally's new beau and Jackson Warren. And she was proud of the way she'd handled herself on the gondola. It took guts to hold Tyler at bay, even though he hadn't really intended to hurt her.

She glanced over at Michael, who was pacing as he talked. He'd shed his insulated jacket and pushed up the sleeves of his black turtleneck. The cadence of his low drawl resonated with determined masculinity. Clearly, he was a man with a mission. She couldn't help admiring his confident stride and his long legs. He reached up and rubbed his hand across his forehead, a casual gesture that emphasized the width of his shoulders.

Staying angry at a man who looked so good wasn't easy. She had an irresistible urge to sidle up beside him, pull the tail of his turtleneck out of his jeans, unfasten his belt and peel off the silk long underwear underneath.

Purposefully, she looked away. Her anger wasn't really directed at Michael. She was mad because they weren't going to be together. There had never been a promise for anything serious. She'd known the terms last night when they slept together and had thought she could handle a no-strings-attached affair. But she just wasn't made that way.

He entered her field of vision. Taking a position on the other side of the coffee table, he closed his cell phone. "Deputy McGraw's a good man."

She recognized his attitude. This was the professional Michael. The former Marine and homicide detective. The man who got things done and took no prisoners. "You spoke to McGraw?"

"He's going to bring Tyler in to identify Jackson from a photo array, but that's just a formality. McGraw will notify the CBI immediately. They'll start surveillance at the airport and then circulate Jackson's photo to the local hotels."

"A manhunt," she said.

"That's what I'm hoping for." His posture was stiff, as if he were standing at attention. "You might as well settle in, Brooke. We have to wait for McGraw to call me back."

She opened her mouth to object. He had, once again, made plans without consulting her. But there was no point in arguing with the commander. He reminded her of a general addressing his troops before they went into battle. Powerful. Strong. And incredibly sexy.

"I spoke with the feds," Michael said. "They're on board."

"You sound pleased with yourself."

"I'm pleased with you," he said. "You're the one who figured it out. Good work."

"Yes, sir." She snapped off a wry salute. "I did my best work, sir."

He arched an eyebrow. "Are you smarting off?"

"I'm trying to."

Without a word, he went to the fireplace and flicked a switch. Instantly, electric flames danced along the surface of the logs. She watched suspiciously as he disappeared into the kitchenette. When he returned he was carrying two tumblers of bourbon, one of which he placed in her hand.

"I believe you deserve a toast." He lifted his glass. "As my uncle Elmo often says, 'Here's to fair weather, fast horses, fine women and a bluetick hound named Jo-Jo.'"

He clinked his glass against hers.

It would have been rude not to take a sip. She wet her lips and allowed a tiny portion to slide over her tongue. Bourbon wasn't her favorite drink, but this blend tasted smooth and rich. "To Jo-Jo."

He peered at her over the rim of his glass. "And here's to Brooke. The smartest, bravest woman I've ever known."

"What about beautiful?"

"Without doubt, the most beautiful woman I ever knew."

She realized that he was already speaking of her in the

past tense. She was a woman he knew once. Not somebody who was still around.

Joining her on the sofa, he reached down to unfasten his hiking boots.

"What are you doing, Michael?"

"As long as we're waiting for McGraw's call, we might as well get comfortable."

His jade eyes held a distinctly sensual gleam. It didn't take a genius to figure out what he'd like to do, and she wasn't opposed. Making love with Michael was amazing—her body was already quivering in anticipation.

It could be the last time. As soon as Jackson was taken into custody, Michael would leave her. She might be driving a dagger deeper into her heart by letting him touch her again.

He kicked off his boots and reached for hers. She pulled her feet away. "You don't always get to have things your way."

"What are you saying?"

"No. I'm saying no."

He leaned closer. He started to take the glass from her hand, and she snatched the bourbon back and drained it in two shuddering gulps. Heat from the strong liquor spread through her. "Michael, don't."

"When you got dragged away from me," he said in his low, slow baritone, "I nearly lost my mind. I don't think I've ever been so scared. Not in war. Not in pursuit of armed criminals. Not even when I was injured and thought I might die. I don't want to lose you, Brooke."

She wanted to be logical, to explain to him that he couldn't lose something he never really had. They had no obligations, no ties. Their connection was as ephemeral as a snowflake—beautiful, unique and quick to dissolve.

Oh, yes, she had a lot to tell him. But it all boiled down to a simple response. "I don't want to lose you, either."

He came even closer. She could feel the heat from his body. In a whisper, he asked, "Do you want to make love with me?"

"I do, Michael. I mean, last night was beyond anything I ever expected." A delighted shiver rippled through her. "But I can't help having certain expectations about our relationship. If that's what you'd call this thing between us. What do we do tomorrow? Will there even be a tomorrow? Of course, I want you. Yes, I want—"

He cut off her rambling words with a fierce kiss. His arms closed possessively around her, easily overpowering her long-winded rationale.

Willingly, she surrendered. If she only had one more hour with him, only one more day, she wanted as much of Michael Shaw as she could get.

She threw herself into their kiss. As if she'd ever had any other choice.

Chapter Eighteen

Lying on the hotel bed beside Brooke, Michael glanced at his wristwatch. Nearly an hour had passed—a good hour, one of the best in his life. He loved making love to her. It was that simple.

Her reluctance vanished when Brooke gave herself to him, wholeheartedly. A generous woman. An amazing woman. He gazed down at her lovely face. Her cheeks were flushed. Her lips parted. Her blue eyes had that soft, blissful look that came after sweet loving.

With his thumb, he traced a line from her chin, down her throat, past her collarbone to the middle of her naked breasts. He'd like to make love to her again, to spend the rest of this snowy day in bed.

She captured his hand and brought it to her lips.

"Were you really scared?" she asked.

"When?"

"At the gondola. You said that when you couldn't find me, you were scared."

"Nearly went right out of my mind." Someday he might be able to laugh at how he'd been shocked into helplessness, but not yet. He still hadn't quite recovered from it. "That's not how I am. I'm supposed to be good in a crisis."

"Do you remember how it felt?"

"Confusion." He leaned down and nuzzled her ear, hoping to distract her. The questions she was asking seemed headed toward a discussion that he was pretty sure he didn't want to have.

Instead of kissing him back, she pulled up the sheet to cover her breasts. "I've been thinking about how fear feels. Because it's changing for me. I used to be literally paralyzed, but not anymore. You would have been proud of the way I handled Tyler on the gondola. My hands only trembled a little bit. I'm not sure I could have pulled the trigger. But maybe I could have."

"Good thing you didn't. Tyler is our key witness."

The larger issue was taking Jackson into custody. Michael wanted to believe that the combined resources of the Pitkin County Sheriff's Office, the CBI and FBI would succeed in tracking him down. The Atlanta Police Department had failed, but they'd had to search an entire city. Though the Aspen area spanned a vast wilderness, it was small in terms of population.

He checked his watch again, hoping that McGraw would call back soon with a progress report.

"I wonder," she said. "Will my fears ever go away completely? Is it possible to forget? To erase the nightmares?"

He leaned down and kissed her forehead. Her thick, curly hair spread around her on the pillow like an auburn halo. He could feel it coming: the Relationship Talk.

Somewhere between hello and goodbye, most women insisted on this sort of meandering conversation about feelings, hopes and dreams. He always said the wrong thing. The Relationship Talk made him uncomfortable—

like when a woman cried—because he didn't know how to make it better.

Michael preferred a clear plan, a military strategy. First, define the objective. Second, engage in pursuit. Third, achieve said objective.

Hoping to avoid the inevitable, he said, "Relax, Brooke. It's almost over."

"And that's scary on a whole different level." She sat up on the bed with her back leaning against the pillows. "You're going to leave. I'm going to lose you."

"Not necessarily."

"Oh?" Her tone sharpened. "Were you planning to quit the Birmingham police force and move to Aspen to be with me?"

Her attitude was downright aggressive. "Well, look at you. Not scared at all, are you?"

"Thanks to you," she said. "Don't worry, Michael. I'm not going to start making demands or setting up rules. I knew from the start what I was getting into when we made love, and I don't have expectations."

Unsure of where she was headed, he plumped up the pillows and sat beside her. He felt exposed—and not just because he was naked under the sheets. "Go on."

"I'm grateful." She gave him a smile that appeared to be without guile or subterfuge. "You helped me face my fears. I told you my most shameful secrets, and you listened without judging, without making me feel like a victim or a fool."

"I've heard a lot worse. Seen a lot worse."

"This isn't a contest for most devastating trauma. It feels like I'm getting past most of it. The divorce. The abuse. The stalking."

She looked away, and he sensed that there was something more—another secret she hadn't talked about. The smart thing for him to do was back off, let it lie. But he wanted to know what was bothering her. He cared— deeply. "What is it, Brooke?"

"My miscarriage." Her hands rested on her flat belly. "I wasn't far into the pregnancy, still in the first trimester. My baby was a boy. My son. Trevor."

He heard the hurt in her voice. Her loss was something he could understand. Gently, he wrapped his arm around her slender shoulders and pulled her close against him.

"I want a family," she said. "And I want children. The greatest disappointment about my divorce might be that I wasted all that time with Thomas. I'm already thirty-two. It's time I get started thinking about having a family. A child."

"You appear to be in good health. I'd say you've got plenty of time."

"You look nervous." She smiled, studying his face. "Don't worry. I'm not saying that I want a baby with you. I know better. You're not the kind of guy who will ever settle down."

"You're wrong about that. Dead wrong." His gaze sank into hers, and he wondered for half a second if their children would have green eyes like him or blue like her. "Family is real important to me."

"Oh, sure, you've got your sister, mama, Uncle Elmo and Jo-Jo." Her smile broadened. "But that's not the same as having children of your own. Michael, you're a lone wolf."

Though she was letting him off the hook on The Relationship Talk, he wasn't happy about it. He definitely wanted kids of his own. Maybe not tomorrow, but someday.

Before he could put that thought into words, his cell phone rang. He grabbed it from the bedside table. While McGraw filled him in on the current investigation, which included all-out surveillance and canvassing with a photo of Jackson Warren, Michael watched Brooke get out of bed and start putting on her clothes.

The capture of Jackson Warren was imminent. Very soon, Grant Rawlins's killer would be brought to justice.

But Michael wasn't happy.

When he disconnected the phone, Brooke hopped back onto the bed beside him. "Have they got him?"

"Not yet. But it's going to happen soon."

She gave him a sad little smile. "I guess it's almost over."

He didn't want that. Damn it, this was a relationship with a future. *Their* future.

BROOKE TOLD herself that she ought to be pleased with the way things were turning out. With the police on the trail of Jackson Warren, her reputation as a normal person was redeemed—no one suspected her of being a suicidal nutball…or a murderer. Everything was going her way. She'd even convinced Michael that she needed to rescue her vehicle from the hotel parking lot and had driven home in her own car. Soon, very soon, life would return to normal. She should have been deliriously happy.

And yet, a sense of melancholy hung over her like a dark cloud as she bustled around the kitchen, putting together a salad and chicken for dinner. Too soon, her bodyguard would be leaving.

And she was going to miss him.

He held up his cell phone as he came into the kitchen. "They've found the hotel where Jackson was staying. He's not in his room but hasn't checked out."

"Do they know what kind of car he's driving?"

"They've got the license plate. If he's already on the highway, the state police are on alert for his vehicle." He peered through the window. "Looks like its stopped snowing."

"The forecasters say tomorrow will be clear."

Tomorrow might be the day he left. She hoped for a blizzard that would keep him here with her.

"You know how much I hate the cold," he said. "But the new snow is real pretty."

"Should you be standing at the window? Until Jackson is in custody, we should probably stay on high alert."

"You're right," he said. "We should both stay away from the windows."

It wasn't like Michael to not consider all potential danger. He seemed distracted. "What's on your mind?"

"You." He moved closer. "You're on my mind."

He braced his hands on the countertop, trapping her against the cabinets. She liked the way he overpowered her, even liked the way he took charge—sometimes—with his jade eyes gleaming and a devilish grin on his handsome face.

"Don't distract me," she said as she glided her hands up his chest and laced them around his neck. "I don't want to burn dinner."

"When I see you in the kitchen, flouncing around and being domestic, I can't stay away."

"Please don't tell me that you like your women barefoot and pregnant."

"I like you."

He pressed against her, taking his sweet time with a deep kiss that left her breathless. Sensual yearning bubbled inside her. She wouldn't mind running upstairs to the bedroom. Actually, she wouldn't mind ripping off her clothes right here and making love on the countertop.

With a sigh, she said, "We should have dinner first."

"The protein would be healthy," he drawled. "And we can spend all night with dessert."

She managed to serve up the chicken and salad while he opened a bottle of Sauvignon blanc that she'd been saving. While she was digging through drawers, trying to find a taper for the candlestick, she realized that he was the first man she'd cooked dinner for since she moved to this house. After her divorce, she hadn't been looking for a relationship. The opposite, in fact. She'd ignored the men who approached her, never gave out her phone number, never offered anything more than polite, dismissive conversation.

That lifestyle hadn't been unpleasant. If she hadn't had Michael stuck to her side as a bodyguard—if they had never made love—she might have continued for years without a thought of marriage or children.

As they sat at the table, his cell phone rang again. He glanced at the caller ID. "This is odd. I'm getting a call from Tammy Gallegos."

"I'll take it," she said. "I'd like to say hi."

When she answered, a man's voice responded. "Is this Brooke? Brooke Johnson?"

"Yes, it is," she said brightly. "And who's this?"

"You know me. We haven't been formally introduced, but you know me."

She sucked in a sharp breath. Terror washed over her, darkness consumed her. "Who is this?"

"You convicted my brother. You sent him to prison to die like a dog. He was just a kid who couldn't defend himself. You killed him. You. Brooke Johnson. Juror Number Four."

She thrust the phone toward Michael. "It's him."

Michael held the cell to his ear. He stood as if to face the threat. "What do you want?"

She watched as he listened for what seemed like hours. Why was Jackson Warren calling? Why did he have Tammy's phone? Dozens of lawmen from the county deputies to the FBI were searching for him. It didn't seem possible that he was free.

Michael disconnected the call and stuck the phone in his pocket. "We don't have much time."

"What is it? What's happening?"

"He has Tammy. He abducted her from the airport in Salt Lake City."

"That's not possible. She was supposed to leave yesterday. Friday night."

"Which means he had just enough time to grab her and drive back here."

This wasn't right. Tammy was supposed to be in Kuwait, safe with her husband. Brooke pictured the bright, blond woman with everything to live for. "Wouldn't someone notice? Even if she and her husband were on separate planes, he'd know if she hadn't made it on the plane."

"This might be a bluff, but I can't take that chance." Michael was putting on his jacket, preparing to leave. "Jackson said if I'm not at the Aspen Airport in twenty-five minutes, Tammy Gallegos is a dead woman."

"What does he want you to do?"

"Make a trade," Michael said. "Your life for Tammy's."

So he could progress with his serial killings in the proper order? Brooke was the fourth juror, the next on his schedule, the next to die. But did the order really matter that much? It didn't make sense. "This isn't the way he's operated before now. There's no chance he'll get away with this."

"Apparently, he's not aware that he's the subject of a manhunt. He thinks I'm the only threat." He gave her a quick kiss on the cheek. "You stay here."

She couldn't imagine staying here and waiting, watching the clock tick off one slow second after another while Michael faced a serial killer. "I'm coming with you."

"Even if this is a bluff, I can't expose you."

Adrenaline pumped through her veins, driving her to action. She took her jacket off the hook by the back door. "I'm going. If this is a ruse to get us separated, I shouldn't be up here alone. You've said it a dozen times."

He gave her that half grin. "Are you gunning for my job, Ms. Johnson?" His voice was calm though his eyes looked hard, ready for battle. "We'll take both cars. On the way, I'll contact McGraw and arrange for you to meet him."

"If Jackson doesn't see me at the airport, he might hurt Tammy."

"I don't want you anywhere near that bastard."

"But I can't—"

"We don't have time to argue. This is the plan. Take your car. I'll make the phone calls and arrange for you to hook up with McGraw. Then I'll drive to the airport."

She barely had time to nod before he turned off the alarm and went out the door. Taking her backpack, she ran to her car.

"Do you have your cell phone?" Michael called out.

"Yes."

"I'll call you with instructions," he said.

"Got it."

She fastened her seat belt and started the engine. Her headlights slashed through the dark. Though the snow had stopped, the roads would be difficult, and she needed to concentrate on her driving.

When she made the turn from her long driveway to the road leading down into the canyon, she saw the taillights of the Hummer at the stop sign at the bottom of the hill. Michael was waiting for her to catch up.

She heard a roar—an explosion echoed through the valley as a fierce orange light lit up the night. The Hummer was on fire.

Chapter Nineteen

Brooke slammed on the brakes, careening to an icy stop on the narrow road, only a few yards away from the Hummer. She flung open her car door and staggered onto the road. She had to reach Michael, had to help him.

The front bumper of his car was twisted and gnarled. The hood was completely gone, torn from the hinges and thrown to the side of the road. Flames vaulted from the engine, leaping toward the snow-laden branches of the trees. In the glow of the fire, she saw Michael slumped over the steering wheel.

Unmindful of the fiery heat and the danger, she grabbed the door handle with her gloved hands and yanked. "Michael!" She screamed his name. The door was stuck. "Wake up!"

The windshield was shattered and gone, but she couldn't reach him through the flames. She hammered at the driver's side window. "Michael!"

He didn't move.

With all her strength, she pulled at the handle. It wouldn't budge. Maybe the passenger-side door would open. She started around the back of the car.

"Stop."

She whirled in her tracks.

She saw the outline of a dark, hooded figure in front of the car. His eyes glowed red in the firelight. It was him. Stonewall Jackson Warren. Her worst fear had come true.

He laughed. The bastard laughed and said, "It's too late for your boyfriend."

Instinct told her that Jackson was a greater threat to Michael than the explosion or the flames. She had to stop him. The gun. It was in her car.

As she darted back to her vehicle and dove inside, she heard him laughing. "You can't get away from me, Brooke Johnson. This is your fate. Your execution."

Inside her backpack, her gloved fingers closed around the handle. There wasn't time to be afraid. Or to think.

She lunged away from her car. She aimed the automatic, her gaze sighted down the barrel, and squeezed the trigger. She heard the shot. A jolt went up her arm.

"Bitch!"

Had she hit him? She hadn't stopped him. He walked up the hill toward her, his arm thrust out in front of him. She wasn't the only one with a gun.

She ducked behind the open door of her car as he returned fire. Bullets pinged against metal. The window exploded, showering her with bits of glass.

What next? She couldn't think straight. Damn it.

The worst thing she could do was cower and wait for Jackson to step up beside her. Rising from a crouch, she charged up the road. Her hiking boots gave her traction as she dodged left and right.

She heard the gunfire. The muscles in her back tensed. She expected to feel the slam of a bullet piercing her flesh at any second.

"Don't run," he called after her. "I have something to tell you. About Tammy."

For half a second, she hesitated. Had he really captured Tammy? Did he have her stashed away in the trunk of his car? Where was his car?

It didn't matter. She was no good to anyone if she was dead. The best way to help Tammy was to save herself. She couldn't let herself think about whether Tammy—and Michael—were still alive. She had to believe that they were.

Brooke climbed over the snow piled on the shoulder of the road and veered into the trees. Inside the forest, the snow wasn't deep, only a dusting that came as high as her ankles. Underneath, it was icy and hard to maneuver across. Dodging the trunks of tall pine trees, she aimed downhill toward the creek. Her feet skidded. She fell, bounced up and kept moving.

The night cold bit into her cheeks, but she was burning up inside, using every ounce of strength she had. Where was she going? What was her final destination?

At the edge of the creek, she ducked down behind a boulder and peered back through the trees. Though it felt like she'd been going for a long distance, she wasn't far from the road. She could still see the flames from the explosion. They seemed to have lessened. She could also see the trail of her footprints across the new-fallen snow, which pointed to her like an arrow.

Jackson followed her tracks. He was about forty yards away from her, moving slowly. When she saw him earlier today, she'd thought he was physically ill. It looked like she was right. That might work to her advantage.

He paused, bending over to take a deep breath. "Poor Tammy," he said. "You could save her, Brooke."

Her instincts told her that he was lying—the same way Thomas had lied to her, over and over. "You're bluffing," she yelled back.

"Yeah? Then why do I have Tammy's cell phone?"

She wasn't sure how caller ID worked. There was probably a way he could program another phone to show Tammy's name. Or maybe there was a more obvious solution. "You stole it from her."

"Maybe I did." His voice was thin, breathless. She remembered when she first saw him, when he was only an apparition outside the sliding glass door at her A-frame. Even then, he'd been gasping. Maybe the reason he hadn't chased after her was because he couldn't.

"Maybe I saw you and Michael visiting her office in Salt Lake City," Jackson continued. "Maybe I went inside, found her purse and took her phone."

Had he been that close? Had she and Michael passed him on the street in Salt Lake City? All that time, when she'd thought they were safe, he was in pursuit, following her relentlessly.

She raised her gun. If she'd been more experienced, she could have picked him off. But she didn't trust her aim.

The smarter plan would be to circle around, get close enough to him that she couldn't miss. She had the advantage of knowing the terrain and being more agile in the high altitude.

It was time to stop being the victim. She would become the hunter.

HIS EYELIDS pried open. Oily smoke spewed across the dashboard. Michael saw the flames. His vehicle had been disabled by a roadside bomb. He had to move fast, locate the rest of his platoon, and guide his men to safety.

When he reached to unfasten the seat belt, his left arm throbbed. Something was wrong with his wrist. Using his right hand, he pulled off his glove. Swollen. Maybe broken. Not important.

Using his teeth, he yanked off the other glove. He needed full dexterity in his right hand.

Seat belt off, he shoved against the door. It didn't move. He put his shoulder into it. The door hinges squawked and opened. He climbed out on shaky legs. Tomorrow there would be bruises but no broken bones. Good thing he'd been driving a Hummer. He stumbled forward.

Where was everybody? Grant must have cleared the area. Michael could always count on him to do the right thing in combat.

He drew his handgun. Where were the rest of his weapons? His helmet? His flak jacket? He must have come out here alone. Not expecting an attack? He knew better, knew he could never let down his guard. *Make the best of it, Marine. Assess the situation.*

The hammering pain inside his head deafened him to other sounds. Not good. Since he couldn't see the enemy, he'd best be able to use his other senses, to hear them approach.

Focus, he needed to focus. He closed his eyes, tried to clear his mind, to ignore the pain that felt like someone boring into his skull. The cold seeped into his bones. This night was colder than death. It almost looked like he was surrounded by snow, but that wasn't possible. Desert terrain was sand, not snow.

Behind his eyelids, he saw a woman with auburn hair

walking toward him. She held out her hand, beckoning. He wanted to be with her for the rest of his life. He loved her.

She was his mission. He had to keep her safe.

His eyes opened. Where was she? He rubbed his hand across his forehead and felt wetness. Blood stained his fingers. Later. He'd tend to his injuries later.

First, get clear of the Hummer. Those licking flames could hit the gas tank. Put out the fire.

Moving with caution, scanning in every direction, he went to the front of the vehicle. Using his right hand, he scooped up a handful of snow. *Snow. Not sand.*

He struggled to make sense of disparate facts.

He was in Colorado, far away from armed combat. But his Hummer had been sabotaged by a roadside bomb.

He was under attack. But he was alone, without his platoon.

There is no platoon. That was years ago.

He stared at the vehicle. The oily flames leapt higher. This Hummer wasn't military issue. It was black. It was a rental car. He was near a ski resort.

Bits of information fell into place. He remembered Grant Rawlins—Sergeant Rawlins. Grant was dead, murdered execution-style. A wave of grief hit Michael hard. He'd lost his best friend, the man who had saved his life. The reason he was here, in Colorado, was to track down Grant's killer.

But there was something else, some other voice calling to him. There was another reason for him to come back to the present. Someone who needed him.

The woman. Brooke Johnson. He spoke her name aloud, "Brooke."

The mists of confusion cleared as he remembered her gentle smile, the graceful curve of her shoulder. Through the ringing in his ears, he heard her laughter. Brooke was everything to him, the only thing that mattered.

He heard the sharp report of gunfire.

Cradling his injured arm against his chest, he went into the forest to find the woman he loved.

DRAGGING HER feet, Brooke had laid down a clear track that pointed deeper into the forest, knowing that Jackson would follow. Then she doubled back and waited, hiding behind the thick trunk of a tree.

As soon as he went past her hiding place, she'd step out from cover, point her gun and shoot. It was a good plan. Michael would be proud. At the thought of him, panic fluttered in her chest. He had to be all right. He was tough. He had to survive the explosion.

She heard Jackson's labored breathing as he approached, following the trail of her footsteps through the snow. Peeking around the tree trunk, she saw him trudging slowly. Each step seemed to be an effort. He was obviously ill. How did he keep going? What kind of terrible hatred motivated him?

He lurched past her tree, unaware of her presence.

Cautiously, she stepped into the clear and raised her gun. Steeling herself, she aimed at the center of his back, the largest target. She'd taken off her gloves so she could handle the gun. Cold, she was so cold. Her finger stroked the trigger as she prepared to kill a man. He deserved death. He'd already murdered three innocent people… four, counting Sally.

All she had to do was shoot.

Another explosion shattered the moonlit winter night. Startled, she looked back through the trees. The fire in the

Hummer's engine must have reached the gas tank. She saw a ball of flame rising high. No one could live through that inferno. "Oh, God. Michael."

She heard gunfire and felt a heavy jolt against her shoulder. She'd been shot. She dropped to her knees in a heap. Her red blood stained the snow. The gun fell from her hand. She'd waited too long. Her hesitation could cost her everything.

Jackson came into her field of vision. He looked close to death.

"You're sick," she said.

"I got the cancer," he said. "Got my diagnosis on the day my baby brother was killed in prison. I wanted to make my last days on this earth count for something."

"Murder?" What kind of sick, twisted person would want that for his legacy?

"Vengeance," he said.

"Why Sally?"

"The bitch said she'd help me. I was getting pretty weak by then, and I paid her to set you up. We had everything arranged for the hanging. A sedative. The suicide note. The rope." He paused to catch his breath. "Then Sally grew a conscience. She didn't want to kill you."

"I knew she wasn't all bad."

"Bad enough," he said. "The important thing is that I'm still getting what I want."

Brooke thought that she should feel pain from the gunshot wound. Instead, she was dizzy, fading toward unconsciousness. "What about Tammy?"

"She got away. I stole her cell phone but couldn't get her." He coughed heavily. "That's my dying gift to you, Brooke Johnson. You see, I'm not such a bad guy. I'm letting you know that your friend, Tammy, is safe. Now you can die in peace."

Peace? Never. Not for this man who had killed Michael. Her only solace was that she'd join him soon.

Jackson came closer, the barrel of his gun pointed at her forehead. He wheezed and said, "Merry Christmas, Brooke."

Her bare fingers scratched at the snowy ground, finding a chunk of ice. Summoning up all her strength, she bolted upright and flung it in his face.

With a cry, he stepped back.

She struggled to her feet, managing a few steps before stumbling. She braced herself against the rough bark of a tree, overwhelmed by dizziness, fighting to stay conscious.

Several shots tore through the night, but she felt no pain. What was happening? Was she imagining things?

She saw Jackson stagger backward. His arms flailed, but he couldn't stay upright. Blood spurted from his mouth. He sank to the ground and lay motionless.

And then she saw him. Michael.

He kicked the gun from Jackson's lifeless hand and came toward her. One arm wrapped around her waist. "I'm here," he said.

Struggling to keep her eyelids open, she gazed into his face. There was blood on his forehead. Another cut on his cheek. "You're alive."

"I'm never going to leave you, Brooke. I love you."

She must be hallucinating, caught in a dream state between life and death. But he felt solid and real. Hovering at the edge of consciousness, she whispered, "I love you, Michael. I love you."

ON CHRISTMAS morning in Birmingham, Brooke slowly opened her eyes and exhaled a contented sigh after a delicious sleep. Apparently, the cure for her fears and nightmares was to spend every night in Michael's arms.

As soon as the doctors in Colorado said she was okay to travel, they had decided to recuperate at his family's estate in Alabama. The pleasant little guesthouse where they had taken up residence was private yet close enough to the big house that they had all the help they needed. The bullet she'd taken in the shoulder had caused serious blood loss and nerve damage, requiring a sling and exercises twice a day, but she was regaining her dexterity. Michael still wore a cast on his broken wrist. The gash on his head had required stitches.

He came through the bedroom door carrying a tray with their coffee—three sugars for her—and muffins. He set the tray on the antique dresser and checked his wristwatch. "I'm glad you're awake. We need to leave in forty-five minutes."

She sat up on the bed. "Aren't you forgetting something?"

With an easy smile, he leaned down and kissed her. "I'd never forget these lips."

He plumped up the pillows behind her so she'd be comfortable and set up the tray in front of her. Though she still wasn't accustomed to using her left hand, she lifted the coffee and took a sip. "Perfect," she said.

Just about everything was perfect. Though she loved Aspen, the temperate weather in Alabama was a relief. And she liked his family—like Michael, they were an interesting combination of folksy and sophisticated. But mostly she was happy because she was with the man she loved. They'd survived. And succeeded in ending Jackson Warren's sick revenge.

"I have a present for you," he said.

She also had something for him, a gift she hoped he would like. "I might need help. With this arm, unwrapping a package might be more than I can manage."

"You don't need to lift a finger."

He stood beside the huge picture window hidden behind closed curtains. Wearing only jeans and a T-shirt, he wasn't yet fully dressed, and she loved the way the black fabric of his shirt outlined his lean torso. He grinned. "Are you ready?"

She nodded.

"I tried to arrange for snow on Christmas morning, but the weather didn't cooperate."

"Not even for a control freak like you?" she teased.

He shrugged. "Go figure."

He pulled open the curtains to reveal a thick pine tree with every bough covered in artificial snow. He must have done it last night in the dark. So sweet—and endearingly silly. She was touched. "It's beautiful."

He sat beside her on the bed. "I know how you miss your Rocky Mountains. So I also got you this."

He placed an envelope on the breakfast tray. She carefully opened it and pulled out a document. "A deed?"

"For your A-frame house. When we go back to Aspen for a visit, we'll always have a place to stay."

Overwhelmed, she could only stammer, "Wow. I can't believe—how did you—what—"

"McGraw helped in contacting the owner. He still feels guilty about not believing us from the start." Michael sat beside her on the bed and took her hand. "You like it?"

"Love it." With her good arm, she pulled him close and snuggled against his chest, reveling in his familiar scent. He never ceased to amaze her.

He kissed the top of her head. "I'd like to stay in bed all day with you, but we've got traditions. Mama does a Christmas morning breakfast that'll fill you up for the rest of the week."

"But I haven't given you my present."

He grinned.

"Move the tray," she commanded.

She leaned over to the nightstand and opened the drawer. Her heart was beating extra fast as she took out a small velvet box. This was a gamble that might go wrong, but she was going for it anyway.

On the bed, she wriggled around until she was on her knees. She arranged the folds of her cream-colored, silky nightgown—another gift from Michael. Then she held the box toward him. Her gaze melted into his jade eyes. "Michael Shaw, I love you with all my heart. Marry me."

His eyebrows lifted. His jaw dropped. "Come again?"

"You heard me. I figured that if I waited for you to plan the perfect moment to ask, I'd be waiting for a long time. Will you marry me?"

He opened the box, took out the simple platinum band and slipped it on his finger. "I accept your proposal with great pleasure. I love you, Brooke."

"Good. Because I'm pregnant."

His eyes flashed, and he let out a whoop of sheer joy. He lifted her off the bed with his good arm and kissed her hard. "I'm going to be a daddy."

"And a husband."

"I'll never leave your side, Brooke."

"No, you won't."

He laughed. "Who's the control freak now?"

"Let's just say I learned from the master."

"I suppose you did," he said, his jade green eyes shining. She felt fearless with Michael. And she loved it. Almost as much as she loved him.

* * * * *

Silhouette Desire kicks off 2009 with
MAN OF THE MONTH, *a yearlong program featuring incredible heroes by stellar authors.*

When navy SEAL Hunter Cabot returns home for some much-needed R & R, he discovers he's a married man. There's just one problem: he's never met his "bride."

Enjoy this sneak peek at Maureen Child's
AN OFFICER AND A MILLIONAIRE.
Available January 2009
from Silhouette Desire.

One

Hunter Cabot, Navy SEAL, had a healing bullet wound in his side, thirty days' leave and, apparently, a wife he'd never met.

On the drive into his hometown of Springville, California, he stopped for gas at Charlie Evans's service station. That's where the trouble started.

"Hunter! Man, it's good to see you! Margie didn't tell us you were coming home."

"Margie?" Hunter leaned back against the front fender of his black pickup truck and winced as his side gave a small twinge of pain. Silently then, he watched as the man he'd known since high school filled his tank.

Charlie grinned, shook his head and pumped gas. "Guess your wife was lookin' for a little 'alone' time with you, huh?"

"My—" Hunter couldn't even say the word. *Wife?* He didn't have a wife. "Look, Charlie..."

"Don't blame her, of course," his friend said with a wink as he finished up and put the gas cap back on. "You being gone all the time with the SEALs must be hard on the ol' love life."

He'd never had any complaints, Hunter thought, frowning at the man still talking a mile a minute. "What're you—"

"Bet Margie's anxious to see you. She told us all about that R and R trip you two took to Bali." Charlie's dark brown eyebrows lifted and wiggled.

"Charlie..."

"Hey, it's okay, you don't have to say a thing, man."

What the hell could he say? Hunter shook his head, paid for his gas and as he left, told himself Charlie was just losing it. Maybe the guy had been smelling gas fumes too long.

But as it turned out, it wasn't just Charlie. Stopped at a red light on Main Street, Hunter glanced out his window to smile at Mrs. Harker, his second-grade teacher who was now at least a hundred years old. In the middle of the crosswalk, the old lady stopped and shouted, "Hunter Cabot, you've got yourself a wonderful wife. I hope you appreciate her."

Scowling now, he only nodded at the old woman—the only teacher who'd ever scared the crap out of him. What the hell was going on here? Was everyone but him nuts?

His temper beginning to boil, he put up with a few more comments about his "wife" on the drive through town before finally pulling into the wide, circular drive leading to the Cabot mansion. Hunter didn't have a clue what was going on, but he planned to get to the bottom of it. Fast.

He grabbed his duffel bag, stalked into the house and

paid no attention to the housekeeper, who ran at him, fluttering both hands. "Mr. Hunter!"

"Sorry, Sophie," he called out over his shoulder as he took the stairs two at a time. "Need a shower, then we'll talk."

He marched down the long, carpeted hallway to the rooms that were always kept ready for him. In his suite, Hunter tossed the duffel down and stopped dead. The shower in his bathroom was running. His *wife?*

Anger and curiosity boiled in his gut, creating a churning mass that had him moving forward without even thinking about it. He opened the bathroom door to a wall of steam and the sound of a woman singing—off-key. Margie, no doubt.

Well, if she was his wife...Hunter walked across the room, yanked the shower door open and stared in at a curvy, naked, temptingly wet woman.

She whirled to face him, slapping her arms across her naked body while she gave a short, terrified scream.

Hunter smiled. "Hi, honey. I'm home."

* * * * *

Be sure to look for
AN OFFICER AND A MILLIONAIRE
by USA TODAY *bestselling author Maureen Child.*
Available January 2009 from Silhouette Desire.

CELEBRATE
60 YEARS
OF PURE READING PLEASURE
WITH **HARLEQUIN**®!

**We'll be spotlighting a different series
every month throughout 2009
to celebrate our 60th anniversary.
Look for Silhouette Desire® in January!**

Collect all 12 books in the Silhouette Desire®
Man of the Month continuity, starting in
January 2009 with *An Officer and a Millionaire*
by *USA TODAY* bestselling author
Maureen Child.

*Look for one new Man of the Month title
every month in 2009!*

nocturne™

MICHELE HAUF

THE DEVIL TO PAY

Bewitching the Dark

Vampire phoenix Ivan Drake's soul belonged
to the Devil Himself, and he had no choice but
to enforce Himself's wicked law. But when Ivan
was sent to claim the *Book of All Spells* for his
master, he wasn't prepared for his encounter
with the book's enchanting protector. With his
soul already the property of another, would he be
willing to lose his heart, as well?

Available January 2009 wherever books are sold.

www.eHarlequin.com
www.paranormalromanceblog.com

SN61802

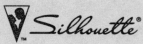

Romantic
SUSPENSE

**Sparked by Danger,
Fueled by Passion.**

Justine Davis

Baby's Watch

**THE
COLTONS**
~FAMILY FIRST~

Former bad boy Ryder Colton has never felt a
connection to much, so he's shocked when he feels
one to the baby he helps deliver, and her mother.
Ana Morales doesn't quite trust this stranger, but
when her daughter is taken by a smuggling ring,
she teams up with him in the hope of rescuing her
baby. With nowhere to turn she has no choice but
to trust Ryder with her life...and her heart.

Available January 2009 wherever books are sold.

**Look for the final installment of
the Coltons: Family First miniseries,
A Hero of Her Own by Carla Cassidy in February 2009.**

Home to Texas and straight to the altar!

THE
TEXAS
BROTHERHOOD

Luke: The Cowboy Heir
by
PATRICIA THAYER

Luke never saw himself returning to
Mustang Valley. But as a Randell the land
is in his blood and is calling him back…
And blond beauty Tess Meyers is waiting
for Luke Randell's return….

Available January 2009
wherever you buy books.

REQUEST YOUR FREE BOOKS!

2 FREE NOVELS
PLUS 2
FREE GIFTS!

♦ HARLEQUIN®
INTRIGUE®

Breathtaking Romantic Suspense

YES! Please send me 2 FREE Harlequin Intrigue® novels and my 2 FREE gifts (gifts are worth about $10). After receiving them, if I don't wish to receive any more books, I can return the shipping statement marked "cancel." If I don't cancel, I will receive 6 brand-new novels every month and be billed just $4.24 per book in the U.S. or $4.99 per book in Canada, plus 25¢ shipping and handling per book and applicable taxes, if any*. That's a savings of close to 15% off the cover price! I understand that accepting the 2 free books and gifts places me under no obligation to buy anything. I can always return a shipment and cancel at any time. Even if I never buy another book from Harlequin, the two free books and gifts are mine to keep forever.

182 HDN EEZ7   382 HDN EEZK

Name	(PLEASE PRINT)

Address	Apt. #

City	State/Prov.	Zip/Postal Code

Signature (if under 18, a parent or guardian must sign)

Mail to the **Harlequin Reader Service:**
IN U.S.A.: P.O. Box 1867, Buffalo, NY 14240-1867
IN CANADA: P.O. Box 609, Fort Erie, Ontario L2A 5X3

Not valid to current subscribers of Harlequin Intrigue books.

Want to try two free books from another line?
Call 1-800-873-8635 or visit www.morefreebooks.com.

* Terms and prices subject to change without notice. N.Y. residents add applicable sales tax. Canadian residents will be charged applicable provincial taxes and GST. Offer not valid in Quebec. This offer is limited to one order per household. All orders subject to approval. Credit or debit balances in a customer's account(s) may be offset by any other outstanding balance owed by or to the customer. Please allow 4 to 6 weeks for delivery. Offer available while quantities last.

Your Privacy: Harlequin is committed to protecting your privacy. Our Privacy Policy is available online at www.eHarlequin.com or upon request from the Reader Service. From time to time we make our lists of customers available to reputable third parties who may have a product or service of interest to you. If you would prefer we not share your name and address, please check here. ☐